# THE SHARDS UNIVERSE

### Real Life Origin

The concept of the Shards Universe stretches back to 1974, when I was a teenager. I'd written two short stories that had the same character; Wendy Rajmir. I used several technologies that grabbed my imagination then and were revisited in later years. Most notably was the MacDonald Phase Unit, which allowed solid objects to pass unharmed through other solid objects. (With horrifying consequences if two phased objects touched each other.) Although Wendy is slated for the Shards Universe, she has yet to make her first appearance. The MacDonald Phase Unit, however, is a critical technology from the year 2586.

The Universe got another shot in the arm around 1980, when I wrote my first Roids Cavanaugh story. Unlike Wendy Rajmir, however, Roids is active now; the wearer of the Red Iron Badge of the Martian Territorial Ranger, a man who epitomized Good and Right during the raucous years of the Martian Iron Rush.

But the Shards Universe truly came to life on December 24, 1995. That was the day I started my first novel, a four book effort entitled, not surprisingly, Shards. A work approaching 300,000 words, Shards quickly became the anchor novel of a Universe that seemingly sprang to life as I progressed into the story. Before long, I envisioned tangent short stories, detailed histories, and societies with a past. And a future. Since all these stories would take place in the same story line and time frame, I unexpectedly had created a Universe!

It was very exciting. And very challenging. Being an avid science fiction reader myself, I understand the importance of details. Details must be accurate, consistent, and plausible! Certainly, there is much,

much more to a good story. But a good science fiction story must include the added attention to detail. And by maintaining my details across many stories, I have a cohesive, believable existence for my characters to live in and their adventures to take place. In other words, a Universe.

As of July 2004, I have nine completed novels, three work-in-progress (wip) novels, a finished novella, and over four dozen short stories. I hope to have much more in the near future. I have two novels published and contracts for eight more. So read the stories I've posted here, buy my stuff as it comes out, wish me luck, and most of all enjoy yourself!

*Pete*
*July 21, 2004*

*Visit http://shardsuniverse.net/*

# *The Science of Magic*

## a collection of short stories
## by Peter W. Prellwitz

To Chris,
It was great meeting
you. Hope you keep
writing!

Peter W. Prellwitz

May 29, 2010

**The Science of Magic**

Copyright © 2005 Peter W. Prellwitz

**Double Dragon Press**

Published by
Double Dragon Publishing, Inc.
PO Box 54016
1-5762 Highway 7 East
Markham, Ontario L3P 7Y4 Canada
http://www.double-dragon-ebooks.com
http://www.double-dragon-publishing.com

ISBN: 1-55404-231-3

Book Layout and Cover Art by Deron Douglas

Science. Magic. Both sources of unimaginable power. All that prevents ultimate control, and thus ultimate power, is that science and magic do not exist in equality in the same dimension.

Until now.

It is the thirtieth century, and mankind has learned a new kind of programming. Pentrinsic code, which uses zeros, ones, twos, threes, and fives, runs on a three-dimensional platform: reality. Running a pentrinsic program results in a warping of realty. In other words, magic.

But still science had the superior position, for learning to "cast" even the most basic pentrinsic program took decades of study.

Until now.

Kerri Marks was born of human parents, but she is also the first of an entire race: *Homo Magicus*, an offshoot of mankind born with the inherent ability to understand and use pentrinsic code. Other children with this powerful, inherent gift are born. And so a race is born. But their numbers are low. They are young. They are not organized. They do not have a way to express their raw power, this blend of science and magic.

Until now.

# POP QUIZ

*October 12, 2953*

Miss Hennessy had always been pretty, Kerri decided on the first day of school. She was pretty in their normal classroom in the puterverse, where her brilliant pinks and glowing blacks always excited the children with the way the colors wrapped and floated around her body. And now that Kerri was seeing her in real life for the first time since school started two months ago, she was even more pretty than in the puterverse. With a keen child's sense, Kerri could see Miss Hennessy as she looked when she was a little girl like her: small frame, brown hair, blue eyes and even the same smile, with the same missing front tooth, the grownup tooth not quite ready to show.

Kerri Marks had only been in school for two years; but at the age of six, she was quite certain no one was as nice and wonderful and pretty as her teacher, Miss Hennessy. And now they were in the same room!

"All right, children!" Miss Hennessy said in a firm voice that she softened by a smile. "Let's all have a seat on the floor and introduce ourselves properly. I'm just as eager to know you as you are to see me." She sat down on the floor and carefully spread her long skirt out just perfect. The nine children; bouncing around only seconds before, hurriedly settled down, sitting on the soft, warm floor around her. Kerri was very happy to see that she got the spot next to Miss Hennessy, on her left. Miss Hennessy gave her a warm smile that made Kerri want to tell her absolutely everything about herself; but she did not, knowing her teacher always did things just so. The last of them quieted, and all bright eyes looked up at her.

"Very good!" Miss Hennessy said happily. She looked them over carefully, and if anything, she was even happier with what she

saw. "My! What lovely children you are! Bret, stop poking Maggie."
Bret's hand immediately jerked back, and Maggie gave him a quick
smirk. "Maggie, you don't need to do that. Well! I know you've been
my pupils for two months now, but we've only met in the puterverse.
Since I'll be here on Coda for the next three weeks, we can do this
properly. Please stand up and introduce yourself. Tell me how old
you are, what you like the most, what you don't like the most, and what
you'd like to be when you grow up. Victor," she said to the boy on her
right, "we'll start with you."

Victor jumped to his feet and looked at his classmates, then at
Miss Hennessy.

"My name is Victor Lu and I'm six and I like wiener dogs an'
Codan jump birds an' I don' like girls!" he said proudly, then blushed,
"'cept you, Miss Hennessy. An' my mom. An' my sister, too, but only
'cause my mom says I have to. An' when I grow up, I'm gonna be a ball
chaser pilot like my dad!" He sat down, certain no one could top his
performance. The girl beside him stood.

"My name is Hana Yoshigawa. *Hana* means 'flower' in the lan-
guage of my ancestors," she said proudly. "An' I like flowers and the
color blue and I don't like boys!" she said sternly, stomping a foot at
Victor, who laughed and buried his face in his hands. "And when I
grow up, I wanna be an astro-namener, like my mom AND dad!" she
concluded, satisfied Victor had been bested and seated herself with a
flounce on the floor. Suddenly remembering, she jumped to her feet.
"And I'm six years old!" she shouted and then sat down again.

One by one the others took their turn until at last Kerri stood
up. She had her hands folded behind her jumper and twirled back
and forth, her pigtails flopping against her small back.

"Hi. My name is Kerri Marks and I'm six years old. Umm . . . ."
She giggled and looked at Miss Hennessy, who smiled reassuringly.
"Oh, yeah! I like my Uncle Paul and I like being in school and I like
making things pretty. I don't know what I don't like. Broccoli, I suppose, only just a little. And I want to be a muser when I grow up, like
my great grampa Marks was. Only maybe I want to be a teacher, too."
She sat down.

"Thank you, very much, children. That was nicely done. Shall we get started with today's lesson?"

"But you didn't say anything about yourself, Miss Hennessy!" Victor accused.

"You're right, Victor. I shall take care of that right now. My name is Deborah Hennessy and I'm . . . ."

"You gotta stand up, Miss Hennessy!" Megan and Donny both said.

"All right!" she laughed and stood up. She bowed to them. "My name is Deborah Hennessy and I'm twenty-six years old. I like children and I like teaching and I like Begorian soul music. I don't like broccoli, either." Kerri's heart jumped, and she suddenly thought that being a teacher was better than being a muser. "And since I'm already grown up, I'll say that I'm happy to be a teacher and very happy to be your teacher." She clapped her hands. "Now! Who knows why we're meeting here today, instead of in the puterverse classroom?" Hands shot up excitedly. "Yes, Donny?"

"You're gonna show us penters . . . prentis . . . you know! Magic!"

"That's right, Donny. But who knows the name? Kerri?"

"It's called Pentrinsic code, Miss Hennessy," she said precisely.

"That's right. And do you know why we're not in the puterverse?"

"Uh-huh," Kerri said eagerly, happy to be the font of wisdom. "'Cause the puterverse is binary and trinary code, an' pentrinsic codes gots threes an' fives in it, sorta, so it won't work there!"

"Well, I'm impressed, Kerri!" Miss Hennessy exclaimed. Kerri beamed. "How is it that you know so much about pentrinsic?"

"That's because I like it and my dad does it and so does my grampa and gramma." She took a deep breath, then burst out, "I can do some, too!"

Miss Hennessy blinked a couple times, then nodded for her to sit down, which Kerri did, still glowing with pride.

"I'm sure one day you will do some, Kerri. But that's only for older people, who study very hard. In fact, that's why we're going to talk about it today. Even though it might be ten years, each of you could one day code magic!" They all stared wide-eyed at her, not so much at the thought of becoming musers as much as at the incredible amount of time she'd said. Ten years! She smiled understandingly and tapped an access button, raising up a hologram of a blue and green planet in their midst.

"Who can tell me what planet this is?"

"Halo!"

"No, it's not! Where's the rings? That's Deerkin!"

"Huh-uh! That's Nojura!"

"Halo!"

"Soso!"

"Mant!"

"Imdlemodin!"

"Earth!"

"Halo!"

"Wait! Children! Wait!" Miss Hennessy held her hands up, only narrowly averting open hostilities. "Someone was right, though I suspect it was a guess. That's Earth. Let me tell you about it.

"A long time ago, almost a thousand years, Earth was the only place that humans lived. Then we learned how to travel through space and started finding planets like the ones you called out and started living on them. The planets are all different. Halo has eight rings. Mant is a very hot planet, and Nojura is almost all water. Soso has no moons, and Imdlemodin has five. And our planet, Coda, has such clear air that we can see stars even after the sun comes up.

"But they all have things in common, too. They all have air we can breathe and plants we can eat. They all have animals, both wild and tame. They all have weiner dogs." Victor shouted yay! causing Miss Hennessy to force down a smile. "And one other thing, too, children, they all have magic. In fact, the entire universe has magic. Except Earth."

They all looked suddenly sad and gazed in pity at the solid hologram that rotated slowly inside their circle.

"How come?" Hana said in a quiet voice.

"We don't know, Hana. That's just the way it is. Scientists keep trying to understand why, but haven't found the answer." She nodded her head and the hologram flashed out.

"What we do, know, however," she added with a cheerful note, "is that pentrinsic code does work here. A muser can write code on reality, changing it. Some use it for healing. Others use it for fixing and working with machines. Some use it to protect us in case we are attacked, though that hasn't happened for almost a hundred years now. And some use magic for teaching it to others." She fell silent.

What she said slowly dawned on the children. They began gasping and smiling, their eyes widening even further as they stared at Miss Hennessy, the absolute center of all their attention.

She moved her hands close together and made an imaginary ball. The children watched in stunned fascination as Miss Hennessy's hands moved faster and faster. Within her hands, they imagined they could see the ball. She whispered a brief word that they didn't understand and suddenly moved her hands apart. Their faces went from wide-eyed to bug-eyed.

Floating in the air where her hands had been was a flashing blue and red ball! It smelled like chocolate and bright white flowers. It hummed and sang a soft song, tickling their insides lightly and making them feel safe and happy.

"This is called a Haven spell, children," Miss Hennessy explained, not at all perturbed that they continued to stare at her glowing ball instead of her. "It can be used to make you feel better when you're sad or if you're a little sick. There are stronger and larger haven spells that will do even more. And the Haven spell is one of only hundreds of other spells. One day, if you work and study and practice, you might be able to cast this same spell and make your friends feel better."

Kerri stared at it, mouth opened. She'd seen her Daddy do magic all the time, but he was the town muser. He was supposed to do magic. But Miss Hennessy was a teacher! And she could muse! Kerri didn't have to choose between being a teacher or a muser. She could be both, like Miss Hennessy! To Kerri, the world suddenly became an even brighter place than it had been before.

Miss Hennessy moved a gentle hand across the ball, and it faded out, causing the children to immediately ask for her to do it again. She laughed but shook her head.

"Sorry, but I'm much more a teacher than a muser. I can only cast one or two small spells a day before I'm too tired. Now, let's see what we've learned. Who can remember the name of the code?" Hands shot up. "Greg?"

"Peterisic. I mean . . . Pen trin sic," he answered, nodding his head with each syllable.

"Very good. And what can it . . ."

"You can call it magic, too," Hana pointed out.

"Yes, you can, Hana. Pentrinsic code and magic are the same thing." Miss Hennessy eyed her with a brief stare, only slightly less soft than normal. "But you should not interrupt."

Hana slapped her hands over her mouth. "I'm sorry, Miss Hennessy!" she exclaimed through her fingers.

"That's all right, Hana. So, children, what can Pentrinsic code— or magic—be used for? Megan?"

"For healing!"

"Yes. Kerri?"

"For working on machines."

"That's correct. Victor?"

"For blowin' stuff up!" He emphasized his point with several sound effects.

"Almost, Victor. We use it for defense, but only when necessary. Good! Now, answer this question: where is the one place you cannot use magic?"

"Earth!" three or four of them shouted.

"Good! And for the last question: which of these three planets is Earth?"

The children looked at the center of their area, waiting for the three solid holos to appear, but it remained empty. Miss Hennessy frowned, then turned her head slightly, quickly accessing the puterverse.

"Hello? Yes. This is Miss Hennessy from the Itinerant Teachers Association. I'm conducting a class on Coda and seem to have lost partial phased access. Could you . . . thank you so much!" She turned her head back to them, ending access and smiled.

"Sorry, children, but the building's access grid is acting up again. Puterverse repair says it'll be about five minutes until I can bring up the holos. In the meantime . . . " she broke off. "My! That was quick! And such incredible quality, too!"

Floating in front of them were three planets: one more blue than green, another more green than blue, and another almost entirely blue and sporting a thin ring. Each had moving clouds patterns and even showed the glistening of their respective, unseen suns reflecting off the water surfaces. The hemispheres removed from the light were cast in the dark of night. Everyone could see the pinpoints of light that indicated cities.

The kids started chattering, pointing at the vibrant and highly detailed images, but Miss Hennessy shushed them.

"These are the best constructs I've ever seen! I still need some-one to tell me which one is Earth, however. Victor?"

"Ummm . . . it's this one!" He pointed to the blue planet with the thin ring.

"No, Victor. That's Nojura. Why don't you try, Kerri?"

"I can't, Miss Hennessy," Kerri said.

"Yes, you can, Kerri. Try to remember what I said about Earth; then use that knowledge to pick the correct planet."

"No," Kerri said, shaking her head, "I mean I can't pick 'cause it wouldn't be fair."

"Why not, Kerri?"

"'Cause I made the planets appear, an' so I know which one is Earth already," she said simply.

The children giggled, but Miss Hennessy suddenly looked thoughtful. Still looking at young girl, she accessed again.

"Yes . . . this is Miss . . . no, no, I'm not complaining. Yes, I'm sure you're working as quickly as possible. I hate to sound silly, but is the interface already up by chance? No? I see. Thank you." Her eyes readjusted to real light, and she took Kerri by the hands. The others were quiet.

"Kerri. Child. Listen very closely. Did you make these planets?"

"Uh-huh," she nodded, now not at all certain she should have. She suddenly burst out, upset at displeasing her most favorite, favorite teacher. "I'm sorry, Miss Hennessy! I just wanted to help! I'll make them go away! I promise!"

She turned back to the images and motioned her hands in stuttered rhythm. One by one the planets popped out of sight, leaving behind a gentle aroma of baked bread and fresh grass.

She turned back to her teacher, feeling very guilty. Miss Hennessy, seeing the girl's distress, smiled at her.

"Don't be sad, Kerri. What you just did is impossible. Hopelessly, incredibly, wonderfully impossible!" Kerri's eyes began to brighten in realization that she'd done something very good. She began twirling back and forth with embarrassed pride.

"I just wanted to be like a teacher, like you, Miss Hennessy. And a muser, too," she said. "And I want to be just like you, too!" she blurted out.

Miss Hennessy, her view of the world abruptly and joyously jarred, gave a happy laugh and held her arms out to her pupil, who ran into them.

"Kerri, I think you'll be a very good teacher some day." She patted Kerri's head and straightened her pigtails. "And I think your students are going to learn more than they ever dreamed possible!"

# THE THIRD COROLLARY

*October 23, 2965*

The classroom was all abuzz when Kerri arrived. She'd been held up in the puterverse when the overloaded access of billions of people eager to find out the fate of the *Lynx* forced Efwon—the puterverse's ancient guardian—to carefully restrict entering and exiting. She'd always been lucky whenever puterverse overload triggered Efwon's involvement, being among the first on and first off. But the sheer volume of access this time was such that she still had to wait fifteen minutes to get off. It would have been easier for her had she still attended classes in the puterverse, as she had for the past fourteen years. It was required, however, that all juniors and seniors wishing to join the Itinerant Teachers Association attend live instruction their final two years.

The babble from the classroom, belied the actual attendance, though; and Kerri breathed a sigh of relief. Of the normal fifteen students, there were only six, counting herself. Not even Professor Westfall had arrived yet. She sank gratefully into her chair and listened in to her schoolmates' conversation.

"I heard they opened fire while the *Lynx* was still in docking approach," Henry, the class know-it-all, said. "Not only were all hands lost, the damage was so severe that the Modins even fried some of their own people when the ship blew."

"I can't believe that, Henry," Theresa objected. Her grandparents were raised on Imdlemodin, and she'd always struggled with her loyalties and beliefs that the planet could be so aggressive. "Where did you hear that?"

"On-verse," Henry replied with a shrug. "My dad is one of Coda's top trinary coders, so I get pretty good access."

"Not as good as Kerri, though," Yuri countered, jerking his thumb at her. "Her dad's only a town muser and he . . ."

"Hey!" Kerri barked. "Watch it, Yuri! What do you mean, *only?*"

"Sorry, Kerri," Yuri apologized quickly and sincerely. "I meant compared to Hank's dad. Everyone knows that your dad's the best muser on the planet. I'm glad he's Hinman's muser."

"Got that straight!" Kerri said firmly, then smiled. "But, yeah, you're right. Dad has great access. Don't know why, but I'm not complaining."

"So what have you heard, then, Kerri?" Theresa asked hopefully. Kerri felt a pang of sympathy for her misplaced hope.

"I'm sorry, Theresa, but Hank's right. I only got off twenty minutes ago, and the reports are confirmed. The *Lynx* was shot down while landing . . ."

"That can't be true!" Theresa interrupted, her eyes getting moist. "Why would the Imdlemodins attack an envoy ship? That makes no sense!"

"War never makes sense," Mikio said in his always quiet, confident voice. "It is a sad but immutable law that society must change to survive. When two societies evolve differently, a contest of will must occur."

There seemed to be nothing to add to that. Fortunately Professor Westfall chose that moment to enter.

"I apologize for the delay, but as you're no doubt aware, the puterverse is backed up for the first time in three years, and I . . ." His eyes lifted to take in the sparse attendance, and he chuckled. "I think I'll stop wasting everyone's time with pointless explanations. We're running nearly thirty minutes late, so let's get started. Please create cordbots. I intend to extend the class today, so be sure to code for a minimum of four hours."

Where there might have been a groan in most classes at the doubling of the period, here there was only grateful acquiescence. Not only were these the very best students in the System, they knew full well the varied lives they would soon lead as itinerant teachers. They had long since come to accept life as it came.

Hands moved in unison, and there came a smell of strawberries and the tingling of chirping birds. One by one, according to their skills, small glimmers of light floated in the air in front of them as they cast their respective recording spells. Soon all had a twenty centimeter image of Professor Westfall suspended in front of them. Each took time to fade out the image colors, leaving only a hazy outline, to avoid distraction.

"Professor?" Kerri called out. Her cordbot was entirely invisible, pulsing into view once every five seconds.

"Yes, Kerri?" He looked around from his instructor's plane toward her and saw her inquiring look. He read it correctly and nodded. "Of course. Yes, could you please make bots for the missing students?"

She nodded and brought her hands up. Envisioning reality around them, she inserted them into the space between mass and vacuum and located the edges. They flashed brilliant pink, releasing the strawberry scent into the air. She tugged at the edges, her slim fingers easily spreading apart the time threads and shaping them into nine small pockets of repeated mass. She turned her head slightly, cocking it to her left, and noticed the audio waves quivering behind the heavier scented threads.

"Ashu doni," she cooed, soothing and coaxing the audio out from behind its temporal curtain. It quieted and peeked out. "That's it. Ashu doni."

The audio thread vibrated free. She wove it into the repeated mass pockets, the audio chirping its pleasure. As she tied them off gently with the temporal curtain, nine images of Professor Westfall instantly slipped from the vacuum of near reality into the classroom.

"Whoa," Henry said impressively, "Nine at once! And in half the time it takes me to do one. Kerri, will you marry me and make us rich?"

Kerri giggled, but otherwise ignored him.

"Thank you, Kerri," Professor Westfall said, "and thank you for not speaking again, Mr. Garland." Henry smiled but was not put off. Being in the ITA required a thick skin, and none of them lacked in that area. The Professor turned back to his plane—crystal clear save where he wrote—and began.

"Cordbot test, test, test," he said in a normal voice.

"Cordbot test, test, test," repeated fifteen high-pitched voices in unison. By the third repeat, they had faded from hearing and were dutifully recording the entire session into memory.

"For the past three months, we've been discussing the second corollary of Woldheim's Spectral Reality Principle. Mr. Nakashima?"

"Yes, sir. The Second Corollary of Spectral Reality states that spectral reality can only exist where mass is present," Mikio responded

"And where there is lack of mass?"

"Lack of mass—or perfect vacuum—is the domain of Illus ional Reality as defined by the Cruz Principles of 2717."

"Very good. You've all come to have an impressive grasp of the Second Corollary. Because of it, your perception of Pentrinsic coding—the rewriting of reality—has also improved markedly, as evidenced by your increased magical abilities. Today we'll continue training by delving into the Third Corollary." He smiled briefly. "A favorite subject of mine. Perhaps you could tell us the corollary, Miss Marks?"

"Woldheim's Third Corollary of Spectral Reality states that time is the expressed existence of mass and can be modified within but not removed from spectral reality."

"And why is that, Miss Marks?" he asked casually. At her silence, he turned back to her and saw her thoughtful frown. "Don't think about it, Miss Marks. We haven't covered that yet, so you have no learned knowledge. Instead, feel for the answer in the same way you use your remarkable skills to cast spells."

Kerri continued to frown. Why couldn't time be removed from spectral reality? Her intuition failed her, for it said that time could be removed. Yet the principle from which the corollary derived was long since proven. She looked up at the professor and shook her head.

"I'm sorry, Professor," she apologized, "but I'm afraid I'm thinking too hard. My feeling for the magic isn't there."

"That's all right, Kerri," he reassured her. "I'm sure that given time, you'll be far more adept at . . ."

From outside their small building there came a deep boom, followed by a drawn out rumble. It faded, but a low, nearly inaudible tone continued on. Abandoning the lesson and classroom, professor and students ran through the door and outside.

Their single room building sat on a small bluff north of the harbor town of Hinman. To the west, the Halivonian Sea, bright blue and clear, rolled quietly into the coast, causing a pleasant crashing sound of waves on the white beaches, but otherwise innocent of noise. The bluff itself was populated only by themselves and a herd of peesh that grazed contentedly at the short grass that covered the rocky land.

"There!" Mikio shouted uncharacteristically. Everyone followed his pointing finger into the sky.

Normally so clear that stars were visible during all but the nooning hours, the sky of Coda was now dotted by dark blotches. Imdlemodin battleships—the very ones their chancellor had denied even having—hovered nearly silent and very deadly. Though still in the upper atmosphere, their size and number diminished the light on the planet's surface, sucking in the suns rays. The air took on an unusual—and frightening—chill.

"They've activated the solar infusers on their ships!" Henry shouted, fighting hard to keep the fear from his voice. "When their cannons reach capacity, they're going to hit us with enough solar energy to ignite a firestorm!"

"No!" Theresa cried, sinking to the ground, her hands clawing at her face. "No! No! No!"

"Where's the Air Guard?" Yuri shouted. His voice contained no fear but only anger. "They should be popping those cruisers like crackers! Why don't they . . ."

"Because there are no pilots, Yuri," Professor Westfall said in a detached voice. They looked at him and saw him staring into a void. "I entered the puterverse to find out that very thing. It would appear the Imdlemodins have discovered a way to keep the puterverse over-loaded to the point that ending access has become quite impossible. I fear I'm in the same predicament. I'm only partially accessed, so I can still speak to you. Other than that, however, I'm quite helpless."

"Those assholes!" Henry spat out. "That's why they shot down the *Lynx*! They knew that it would create a backlog on the puterverse, and they'd be able to lock in everyone, even our military!"

"That is my conclusion as well," Professor Westfall replied. "Would someone please see to Theresa? She seems quite distressed."

"I will," Kerri said, happy to have something to do. She stooped over Theresa and began comforting her.

"No, Kerri." In this moment of crisis, Professor Westfall had started using their first names, hoping to calm them. "I appreciate your caring, but allow someone else. Perhaps Becky?"

"Yes, Professor," Becky cast an attendant haven spell, then helped Kerri lift Theresa to her feet. Both guided the still hysterical girl back inside, the shimmering ball of comfort floating close to Theresa's bent and sobbing form.

"Everyone else should please return to the classroom." Professor Westfall continued to stare out over the sea, blinded and frozen in place by his access. "The situation will be resolved within minutes, I'm quite sure."

"Professor," Henry said reasonably, "being inside or outside will not make one bit of difference when they let go with their solar cannons. And a personal shield works as well here as . . ."

"A personal shield will be no more effective than a putting your hands up, Henry. Please. Do as I say. At least it is warmer in there." He smiled faintly at the irony. "Except you, Kerri. Stay with me." Looking confused, they nonetheless obeyed. Kerri stepped beside him and touched his arm.

"They're all inside, Professor."

"Good. Kerri. I'm sorry to do this, but I must break a confidence and a pledge. As you know, each of your instructors has been made aware of your unique magical gifts."

"Yes, Professor." Ever since the age of six, when she first publicly used the coding powers she'd always had, they'd been explored and investigated but kept pretty much known to only a select few. "You wish me to use them now?"

"Yes."

"I don't know," she said doubtfully. "I can raise a large enough shield to protect us and the class, but not for more than a minute. The firestorm will last at least . . ."

"No. I want you to try to repel the invasion force." He paused. "All of it."

"Professor!"

"You can do it, Kerri!" he insisted. "I'm certain it is only by the grace of God that the timing of this has happened, that Imdlemodin chose today and not yesterday to attack. The proof of the third corollary, Kerri, is a hobby of mine. I've been working on it for years; and it is wrong! I'm certain of it. Your response of only moments ago, your feeling for it, is correct, whatever it is. Use it, Kerri!"

Staggered at his request, Kerri stepped back. Looking around like a cornered rabbit, she sought desperately for escape from this responsibility. There was none. She began hyperventilating, her sharp gasps expelling cloud after cloud. The temperature, a comfortable twenty-five degrees only minutes ago, was now close to freezing.

"Now, Miss Marks," Professor Westfall said firmly.

"Y—Yes, sir," she said, feeling strengthened by his confidence in her. Her hands trembling from the cold, she brought them up in front of her and crossed them.

"Vinanim," she said clearly, straightening her fingers, and then crooking the forefingers. "Anf gaha mo."

The air in front of her opened and laid bare the edges of reality that allowed her to begin coding. Starting at the tips of her forefingers, then spreading quickly to her hands and over her arms, spectral and illusional reality were defined and divided by the young, frightened woman. Sparkling and pulsing, the molecular attraction grid glowed purple with laces of clear orange shooting through it.

Moving her hands into the opened reality that only she could see, Kerri quickly reconstructed the grid, changing the very laws of universal physics. Her deft coding altered the orange laces and changed them to red, allowing for the possibility of mass and energy repulsion. The laces went to deep red, and repulsion became probable. Finally, they faded to purple, matching the exact shade of the grid, and repulsion became a certainty.

"Anf gaha mo," she repeated, instructing the grid to begin expanding. Using the mass of the planet, Kerri was able to feed the grid; but channeling the primary force of gravity through her body was very taxing. She'd only just be able to create a shield large enough to protect them. And the time limit of the shield would be short.

Time. Short. Shivering in the now below freezing temperature, she frowned, forcing herself to think. The feeling was back. The third corollary said time could be modified within mass, but not removed. Her intuition screamed that was wrong.

"Bwant iri mik?" she asked; and the time thread sang out in a high-pitched whistle, bouncing and jumping happily in front of her. She tentatively reached and held it. The thread, seemingly comforted by her loving hand, hummed. But what was she supposed to *do* with it? Overhead, the deep hum had become a loud booming, indicating the imminent firing of the solar cannons.

"Pax," came a voice. It was Henry! He'd come out and was casting a haven spell on her! The cold eased, and she felt a warmth that soaked into her bones.

"Pax." Mikio was beside Henry, re-enforcing his haven spell.

"Pax."

"Pax."

One by one, each student increased the spell. Kerri was now completely encased in a soothing field of safety. Feeling a deep sense of love and belonging, she looked again at the time thread.

And saw the third corollary.

Her heart racing at the beauty of simplicity, she took the time thread into both hands and applied it to itself, folding it and pulling it.

"Pax." It was Henry again. He'd just now come out and cast the haven spell. Knowing he would be unable to cast it twice in one day, Kerri had her proof. He wasn't casting it again; she was reliving the moment.

Quickly, knowing time was slowed but not stopped, she continued pulling and folding the time thread. Inside her, anger flared for the first time. These ships were here to destroy her people and her planet! They had destroyed a ship of peace negotiators, using their deaths as the trigger to war. They were moments from killing millions more. The thread pulled taught, its end coming to a razor sharp point. The coding was complete.

"Y'kaganom inj yut!" she barked, clenching her hands into fists and stabbing the time needle into the repulsion grid.

In a brilliant, blinding flash of utter black, the grid exploded in Kerri's face, throwing her away from the reality breach, causing it to close. The spell had been cast, and the program was running.

Almost at once the rift tore open again, forming black-rimmed pentagons in the air. Dark purple fire roared out from the edges. They continued to multiply, growing in size and number, their protective web rising into the air. Had they not been in the haven's protective shell, it would have killed them.

There was a loud grunt from the professor. The students looked in horror as the pentagons ravaged him. It took only a second for the rapidly expanding web to rise above him; but in the moment it had passed through him, time had ceased to exist for the Professor, and his body was unable to cope. The web—now filling the sky from horizon to horizon—floated free, and he collapsed to the ground, free of the puterverse that only the living could access.

They heard the deep roar above them climax and fall abruptly silent. The cannons were firing! Each ship glinted white, and bolts of burning red poured from them. All over the planet, columns of their sun's energy shot to the surface. The giver of life had been warped by man to be the bringer of death.

But even now the burning web had encompassed the planet and was rising to meet the attack. Crouched around the prone and unconscious Kerri, the students watched as the scorching pillars struck the webbing and ceased to exist, disrupted from the time stream and torn from their reality. The webbing had absorbed and obliterated the attack but was still not satisfied. Continuing upward, the webbing reached the top of the planet's atmosphere and began ensnaring the cruisers. One by one, each ship was caught in the web and destroyed utterly, with not even its explosive death throes left behind as testament to their existence.

Its hunger finally appeased, the webbing faded in strength and was soon lost from sight as the program came to an end. In its wake, the skies sparkled pure and clean and unspoiled by the hand and hatred of man, horrifically purged by the grasping of an idea, the proving of an insight.

The third corollary finally understood in its awesome completeness.

# STUDENT OF THE LESSON

*October 30, 2981*

"Ma'am?" came the tentative voice from across the class. The classroom was very unusual, a massive, empty warehouse 200 meters square and with a roof over fifty meters above. The class itself was located in the center of the expanse and had no furniture, no books, no study aids of any kind. Just five students and their teacher, Major Kerri Marks.

Kerri turned away from Lieutenant Vager's musing field and fixed her eyes directly on the source of the voice, as though seeing straight through the woman and deep into her soul. The class was composed of advanced musers all over the age of twenty-five and all with five or more years of front line magical attack experience. It was nonetheless disconcerting for all of them to see a blind woman so easily and accurately pin them down with her beautiful yet unseeing eyes.

"Yes, Lieutenant Collins? Are you having difficulty with your Immobilize spell?" Kerri walked toward the woman, deftly avoiding the two students in her path. It was rumored that Major Marks could actually hear the threads of mass and time as they fluctuated and bent around spectral reality and that they could move according to what they told the thirty-four year old woman who had revolutionized the art of magical warfare.

"Yes, ma'am. I can cast the field over an area of nine thousand cubic meters, and it effectively freezes every leg joint of any enemy caught within the field; but as soon as someone else enters the field—friend or foe—the spell is disrupted."

"Yes, that is a problem, though not a serious one. You would be unable to maintain the spell in the event of a rush. Nor could you use it as a trap, but it would still be useful in the case of a pinned force. I wouldn't worry, Lieutenant," she reassured the woman. "Casting time is less than five seconds and being caught in the field for even an instant is painfully debilitating for hours."

"But how can I fix it, ma'am?" Collins persisted. "I want maximum crippling effect and be able to maintain it in multiple scenarios."

Kerri sighed. Sixteen years the Four Planets had been at war with Imdlemodin and Charth, and still they only wanted to kill. When would the nightmares end—literally for her and her students—and everyone would realize how tired they were of war? Sadly, the weariness of war had gone nearly a full generation now and had dulled their awareness of there ever having been another way.

"I can teach you how to enhance the field, Lieutenant, but you run the risk of physical damage to yourself." She touched her own face briefly, indicating her eyes. "Do you really want . . ."

Her conversation was cut off by a loud shout as dozens of armed soldiers poured in from all four sides of the warehouse.

"Evasion attack Theta Two!" Kerri barked instantly. "Repulse and ensnare!"

There were five silent shimmers as every muser except Kerri disappeared, slipping into a spectral warp. Their physical mass changed into temporal mass and allowed them to relive a single nanoecond of time a trillion times over. They moved unseen and instantly to optimum attack positions.

The attacking force staggered as a whole at the unexpected vanishings, but pressed on toward Kerri, the primary prize in the raid. She stood quietly, waiting for them, drawing them in to give her students the best possible advantage.

When the first dozen attackers had closed to within ten meters, she bent down and gently laid her hand on the ground. The planet's mass under her fingers organized itself into circular patterns, each earthen graphic encased in vacuum.

"Din na gote," she said calmly.

Up shot a Vacuum Shield that encased Kerri. It shimmered blue and green as reality bounced off it; then abruptly turned yellow as it expanded out rapidly. It struck the closest ones, and they were tossed roughly back, their inertia magically reversed.

The attack broke, and the columns of rushing soldiers quickly turned into a restless, disorganized mob. Their confusion was further compounded when half of them suddenly slumped to the ground, all their mass transferred to their skulls. The effect was harmless but nonetheless incapacitating.

Down to about fifty effectives, orders were shouted to withdraw. Those that could instantly obeyed, but went no more than two steps before they too staggered about, intoxicated to the point of incoherent thought.

Within moments, Kerri's students had disabled an entire company. Turning in a slow circle, Kerri listened carefully for any further threat. The vacuum was humming in one corner of the warehouse, bouncing around an object two meters in height and suspended twenty meters above the floor. The mass threads passed by without a murmur, telling Kerri exactly what she needed. Giving a small smile, she eased open a reality rift in front of her, selected three time threads and four mass threads. Running her fingers down their lengths, she gave a soft sigh and then withdrew her hands. The vacuum was still bulging, but the pulse was much calmer now.

She finished her inspection of the battlefield and was satisfied. She canceled the Vacuum Shield and began working her way to the north end of the warehouse, nimbly stepping over or around the prone or staggering soldiers. Her students reappeared from various positions within the groaning and babbling field and began casting haven spells, healing and setting to rights the damage they'd wrought.

"Looks like that's thirty-eight straight, Colonel," she called out. Standing just outside the warehouse, in the dim overcast light of Nojuran skies, was Colonel Steven Wilcox. When he gave no answer, she gave a humorless smile and pointed toward the vacuum bulge. "It *is* over, Colonel. Your cloaked muser is off in dreamland right now, and will be for another hour. Nice try, though."

Only upon hearing that he did give a derisive snort, telling Kerri he'd conceded.

"I thought I could catch you this time, Major, what with the class distraction, the sheer volume of men and Lieutenant Silverberg slipping in during the rush." She felt his smile from twenty meters. "I will get you sooner or later."

"Perhaps."

"Another day, though," he said. "Right now, the General wants to see you. He said to send you down after you'd kicked my butt." He laughed. "Guess that's why he's the general. He called it from . . ."

"Hostile!" came a shout from Lieutenant Collins, standing thirty meters behind and to the right. Kerri whirled instantly and formed a Vacuum Needle ready to launch. Her hearing picked up the sudden movement on the ground, and the ripples of reality against her skin told her the entire story. An Imdlemodin had infiltrated the unit and was making a suicide attack. He'd remained motionless after being cured by the haven spell, drawing Collins in closer. When she'd bent over him to see what was wrong, he'd pulled a gun and fired, giving her only enough time to alert the others.

Reality split open in a one-dimensional line between Kerri and the assassin, and she forced the Needle down the channel using the planet's gravity as propellant. As Collins fell back from the assassin's laser shot, blood flowing from chest and back, the Vacuum Needle stabbed into the Imdlemodin. He screamed as Kerri explosively expanded his insides with non-reality; then sighed and collapsed dead as she canceled the sphere, allowing the crushed, ruined organs to puddle onto his shattered spine.

Collins' fellow students gathered around her instantly, casting the Healing and Haven spells magic seemed made for. There was a dreadful pause while their efforts went unrewarded; then Kerri sensed a sudden easing of tension.

"She's going to make it, Major," Lieutenant Vager said in his deep, comforting voice. "Another two centimeters down, though . . ." he trailed off, leaving the sentence unfinished.

"Thank you," Kerri replied. Hatred for the attack and concern for her student put an odd tone into her voice. "See to her comfort, please. I'm going downside to speak with the General." She turned to

Colonel Wilcox and gave him a sightless gaze that froze his soul.

"Colonel," she said very precisely, "I suggest you increase your screening procedures. I'd hate to see my students become jumpy during drills. If they are distracted by the fear of actual assassination attempts, they'll be unable to keep proper focus on their spell casting. We would end up doing the Imdlemodin's work for them." She walked by him stiffly and moved unerringly toward the cloaked entrance to their underground base. She and Wilcox had been friends for over ten years, but Kerri always put her students first.

*\*\*\**

"You wanted to see me, General." Kerri stood at attention in front of General Harmon's desk. The harmonic angles and deep base tone protrusions his form made on reality showed him to be a big man, heavy with muscle. His fifty-year-old body and mind in combat condition, he moved and spoke with confidence and authority, a leader in the very truest sense. His redolence was heady and slightly sharp, telling her he'd been exercising recently; but he had thoughtfully cleaned up, aware of her greater perceptions for that sort of thing.

"Yes, Major. Thank you for coming. At ease." He called all his officers by their first name, preferring the unwritten discipline of loose camaraderie to the stiff, formalized military dictates. There was enough pressure in real battle. To add the artificial pressure of procedure was ridiculous and dangerous.

His top muser, however, was the exception. To her students she showed care and compassion. Even fondness. To everything else she was very capable and very controlled and very cold. He looked at her well-shaped body and beautiful face and was again reminded how different the inside and outside of a person could be. She'd been like this since her magic had saved the planet of Coda sixteen years earlier, costing Imdlemodin six hundred thousand dead and Kerri—Major Marks—her eyes and her soul. Now those same eyes showed her soul void save for the empty emotion of resolve.

"Stop feeling pity for me, General," she commented, "and tell me what you want my students and me to do."

"They are not students, Major," he said with a clipped tone. "They are attack musers, and you are their commander."

"Yes, sir," she said flatly, both acknowledging and ignoring his correction. "Tell me what you want my squad of attack musers and me to do."

He gave up and went straight to the point. "I'm sending you and your squad through the puterverse on a deep raid into the primary command complex on Imdlemodin. You and your five musers will destroy everything you can in a ten-minute period of time; then any survivors will be brought back through the puterverse."

He expected her to show shock. It was impossible for any-one—musers or otherwise—to travel through the puterverse. Physical entry into a reality that compressed the three dimensions into a single axis meant immediate and violent death. Yet she remained unmoved, except her eyes, which looked straight into his, the icy blue of her irises matching the temperature of her stare.

"I think not," she said simply.

"This is not a request, Major. This is a direct . . ."

"This is a request, General. You want to use my people to test your new unlimited mass transgate technology and make a surprise attack on Imdlemodin. A mission like that cannot be impressed, so I refuse." She gave the smallest of smiles as she sensed the shock intended for her instead coming from him. "I'm fully aware of Nojura's research on using the puterverse to transport living matter. You picked me, General, because you consider me to be the best muser ever. Don't expect me to limit my skills to benefit you alone."

"You are the best, Major. That's why you're going. We need to strike a decisive blow that will rock the Imdlemodin and Charth military to their core." He paused and took a breath. "Major, we're losing the war. Badly."

She'd been leaning slightly forward to drive home her determi-nation, but straightened and took a step back as his comment struck her. That she hadn't known. It weakened her resolve, but she did not break.

"I agree with you then, General. An aggressive risk like this is called for. But you and I both know this is a suicide mission. I should think sending a high yield forced-fusion bomb through the transgate would have a similar effect as six attack musers."

"No. First of all Efwon, the puterverse's guardian, forbids it. Two, not only would it be less effective if sent through, it would also be detected and disabled before detonation. It must be humans, by both design and Efwon's decree."

"Regardless, I can not and will not take this mission." She saluted crisply. "Good day, General." She turned on her heel and made for the door.

"I understand you know a woman named Deborah Hennessy," he said quietly.

Upon hearing the name, Kerri froze, scared and angry, hating him for what he was going to say and hating herself for what she was going to do.

"I do."

"She was a teacher you had some years ago, in your childhood. I believe it was she who encouraged you to become a teacher and who discovered your unique natural abilities with magic. She even resigned from the Itinerant Teachers Association to stay near you in Hinman. I also believe you two stay in touch whenever possible."

"Yes," she whispered.

"Imdlemodin solar attacked Coda last week. They hit your home town of Hinman specifically, targeting it on the anniversary of your devastating defense that nearly stopped the war before it started."

She said nothing, waiting for the blow to fall.

"I'm sorry to tell you that they rained a firestorm on the town, destroying most of the surface structures. Hinman had been able to evacuate for the most part, and they're rebuilding even as we speak. There were over two hundred fatalities, however, and . . . well . . . I'm sorry, Major."

She slowly turned back to him, her eyes tear-filled and burning with anger. She wiped her eyes, her iron resolve shattered; and he felt a pang of regret and self loathing that choked him. "You're a cold-blooded son-of-a-bitch, Thaddeus," she said.

"Then you are my heartless mother, Kerri," he replied, his voice a razor edge burred by sincere love. "I was your first student fifteen years ago, and you made me into an attack muser. I remember the first day. 'I'm going to teach you many things, Thaddeus,' you told me, 'but there's only one lesson to learn.'"

"The cost is high, and everyone pays their measure," she answered.

"And I learned the lesson, the same lesson you learned, Kerri, that horribly glorious day you destroyed the Imdlemodin invasion fleet with a single spell. From the day I became your student, I've paid my measure. I've known nothing but combat when I'm awake and night-mares when I sleep. Your terrible gift has made me into what I am today. Since then, you've trained hundreds of attack musers."

"Three hundred and forty-six," she said tonelessly.

"And how many are alive today?"

"Eighty-one, damn you," she choked out, wincing in deep pain.

"Eighty-one," he repeated. "And all of them owe you their lives and their abilities, Kerri. You taught them—and me—how to use magic to attack. You taught them to be students of the lesson. And because of that, the Four Planets have been able to hold off Imdlemodin and Charth for sixteen years.

"But the cost! For every attack spell cast, a muser suffers a hundred nightmares. Magic wasn't intended to be used this way, to wreak destruction and death. So you and your students pay the price every night. Thousands die, tens of thousands more suffer and grieve, and evil is held off one more day. All because of your teaching and your gift, Kerri. Your terrible gift. Your unbearable lesson. The Four Planets thank you by day, and I curse you at night."

"All right, we'll go."

He stood, and she sensed his soft smile rippling reality like a gentle kiss and caressing her being with soothing comfort. "I know you will. You'll go because you're a student of the lesson you teach. You and your students will pay your measure, and theirs. More will die. But peace must be paid for in full so the killing can stop." Again she felt his smile, but there was now sorrow woven into his comfort.

"You taught me that."

AUTHOR'S NOTE: A history of the Six Planets War and what happened on that raid—as well as the impact it had on society in the fourth millennium, is recorded in the novel *Diminished Heroes* by Peter W. Prellwitz

# SOLDIER'S BURDEN

*Monday, May 30, 3014*

"Hurry up, Kerri, or we'll be late!" Ruth's patient voice, the edges a trifle ragged with annoyance, came through the bedroom door. Straightening her dress uniform, Kerri Marks smiled at her friend's need to always be on time. Kerri stood in front of a mirror, but it was quite pointless: Kerri had been blind since early adulthood. Still, the reflective glass made for a useful surface for her Image spell, and she could visualize a perfect image of herself from it. Sixty-seven years old, she nonetheless carried herself as a woman twenty years younger. Her uniform, both despised and cherished, was crisp and clean, a symbol that told all who she was, though she'd never actually worn it while in the service.

Connecting the final campaign braid to her shoulder, Kerri canceled the image spell and walked to the door. The solid energy anticipated her exit and shut off soundlessly.

"Finally!" Ruth said.

"Now, now, Ruth." Even though her companion was in her mid-thirties and a competent soldier by her own right, Kerri nonetheless chided her gently. "We both know you always set aside an hour to travel to Hinman, and it only takes twenty minutes. I'm sure we'll arrive in plenty of time."

"Not if we get attacked on the way, like last year."

Kerri shook her head. "We're safe this year. He won't attack until about ten minutes into the ceremony."

Ruth nodded, accepting her friend's foresight as a reliable source. Though Kerri could not predict the future, she saw reality in a unique way that allowed her insight at many levels. To Kerri, the future was strands of the present that extended forward, dim but discernible.

Ruth made a mental note of the warning, her hand touching the discreetly hidden fusion pistol she always carried to protect Kerri.

They walked quietly through the comfortable home—a gift from a grateful planet—and outside to the waiting hov. They got into the vehicle—Kerri in the back while Ruth drove—and headed off to the harbor town of Hinman. It was a typically bright spring day. Several dozen stars glimmering, competing with Coda's own white sun. Kerri could not see the beauty, though. The gentle warmth of the sun only reminded her of that horrible day a decade earlier. That horrible day that the Six Planets War had ended by her own hand.

\*\*\*

Scott was coughing up far too much blood. Kerri increased the potency of her Haven spell. A cloud of soft blue glimmered around them, drowning out the gunfire that pummeled the small bunker they were in. Beside them were the smoldering remains of the traitor, the cause of Scott's approaching death.

"Sorry, Kerri," he choked out, breaking into another fit of coughing. "He was faster than I thought possible. Broke through my shielding before I was set up. I . . ."

"Hush, Scott," Kerri whispered. His life force gave a shudder in Kerri's mind's eye, and the blood oozing from the four-centimeter hole in his chest darkened. The unstoppable corrosion spell had eaten through an artery. It would be only moments now. "I'm sorry I couldn't get here in time. I'm sorry I couldn't train you better. I'm . . . I'm sorry."

"General Marks," Scott said strongly, mustering his last, "It has been an honor serving with you. I count myse . . . myself fortunate to have known you." His eyes dimmed as he collapsed in her arms. Inside his chest there was a soft pop as the Corrosion spell dissipated, its work complete. The strings of reality that had once been Scott Menbriss veered off from their journey forward into time and scattered and faded as they entered another reality; the reality of death. All that remained were the cold threads of an empty husk.

Seven hundred and seventeen, she thought dully. Scott was the seven hundred and seventeenth student of hers to die. No one but

Kerri knew the exact number, but she would never forget it. Nor would she forget this moment. Five days the six of them had been on the planet of Charth—the Imdlemodin's most powerful stronghold—and now only she was left. And only one option. With six musers, it was hoped they could do a limited atmospheric reduction spell and force the planet's surrender. With only three they could still keep enemy deaths to a minimum. Even two allowed for some control. But now it was only Kerri. Their group had been betrayed from within; and because of that, Charth would bear the full brunt.

She rose quietly, leaving the haven spell glowing over Scott, and exited the bunker. She was immediately targeted by all weapons—physical, energy and magical—but they were unable to touch her. She looked up in the gathering darkness and could feel the pinpricks of reality far above her in orbit around the planet. The invasion force was preparing to land. If they did, the fighting would be prolonged and bloody for her people, and the number of dead would be in the tens of millions. She could cut that number in half, perhaps more; but she would carry the burden for the rest of her life.

A needle of pain lanced her shoulder. She winced and touched it, stopping the bleeding. An enemy muser had managed to penetrate her shields slightly. Kerri looked with empty eyes at the ephemeral strings that pointed back in time several seconds to the point of attack. Sliding her fingers into a pulsing fracture in space, she modified the strings from yellow to clear; then applied a homing beacon. The attack was jolted out of the present and returned to the moment before it was initiated. The muser's death scream and the cessation of pain in Kerri's shoulder happened simultaneously.

Seven hundred and seventeen, but how many enemy musers—students all at some time—had died by her hand? Or died by her students' hands? It must end, no matter what the price to her. Overhead, the pinpricks became more insistent, but Kerri had made her decision.

"Jin ne reath," she said in a low voice. In front of her, reality split into the physical and the ephemeral. Inside the rift was the place that burns.

\*\*\*

"Kerri?" Ruth's soft voice broke into her daymare, bringing Kerri to the present.

"Hmm?" She replied, grateful for the interruption. "Are we here already?"

"Yes," Ruth said, helping her friend from the hov. "We're just outside the amphitheater. They're waiting for you."

"Very well," Kerri sighed, stepping to the ground and standing straight. "Let's get this over with." She shifted her hands slightly and tugged at a small fiber of reality. Instantly, her world went completely dark. Her total awareness of reality around her spooked most people. She purposely closed off her perceptions, deferring to their comfort. "I'm relying on you to watch my back, dear."

"Is that safe?"

"No," Kerri said simply, giving a small smile, "but nothing in life is safe. Still, I can't think of anyone else I'd rather have watching me. Shall we go in?"

Ruth took her suddenly dependent companion by the arm and led her down the gentle path toward the Hinman Amphitheater. More than two centuries old and located just outside the small town, the large outdoor area faced west toward the Havilonian Sea and was used for most public gatherings. The conditioning shield was turned off on this warm, cheery morning; the eternally soft sea breeze brushed the quiet mumble of the respectful crown toward them.

They appeared at the entrance arch, and there was rush of sound as all stood. At least two thousand, all turned toward the woman who had given them this day.

\*\*\*

"Jin ne reath," Kerri repeated. The small opening in reality expanded, and Kerri looked directly into it. "Diw diw str Charth," she commanded, feeling a pang at her heart.

The millions of threads in front of her coiled and molded under her trembling hands. What she was about to do was at once glorious and horrifying. But as is so often the case in war, it is only the hardest of realities that can bring about its end. The strings twirled and spun, and an image of Charth appeared, entwined in both the humming time threads and the alternating emotion rope. She caressed the rope, gently soothing it into a sense of relaxed calm. The attacks on her stopped abruptly as the surrounding area became an idyllic pasture to everyone present, a peaceful glimpse into a new home, free of war and pain and horror and grief.

And life.

\*\*\*

Ruth and Kerri walked quietly down the main aisle to the small podium waiting at the bottom. There was no announcement of her name or her rank. No loud braying of her many military accomplishments, her incredible victories. None was needed. Every person there knew General Kerri Marks, knew what she had done. From the Imdlemodin invasion of Coda, which she had repulsed single-handedly, to the surprise attack on the Imdlemodin command complex at Rangow, to the final battle of Charth—all these were recorded history, required study for upper-tier students. At her behest, though, all remained silent today.

Ruth helped her up the four shallow steps onto the stage and guided her to the podium. Behind her was a closed coffin, a tradition of the day that stretched back countless centuries to its origin on Earth.

Ruth leaned close.

"When?" she whispered.

"Eleven minutes, eight seconds from now," Kerri whispered back. She sensed Ruth's nod of understanding. Ruth released Kerri's arm and stepped back. Kerri felt for the podium and placed both hands on it. She looked out over the crowd, her clear blue, sightless eyes taking in a well of blackness that nonetheless convinced everyone present she was staring directly at them.

She remained quiet, knowing the moment was soaking into their memories, painting the threads of their existence with the crimson warmth of sadly proud recollection. She opened a small corner of her perception and reached her mind behind her, caressing the coffin with her thoughts.  A collective gasp went up from the audience as they watched pink wisps of emotion dance over the polished wooden casket.  Kerri retrieved her gently probing thoughts, her new knowledge both sad and satisfying.  Margaret Taig would represent the dead warriors this day, while Kerri would represent the living.  Though Margaret slept undisturbed in her grave, the coffin behind Kerri contained Margaret's second uniform and fusion pistol.  Margaret had been a valiant daughter of Hinman, having died in combat on Imdlemodin four years before the war had ended.  Kerri had only known her briefly—way back when they were  six-year-old students—but she was in a deep sense closer to Maggie than she was to those who hadn't been there, to those who hadn't been to the place that burns.

She turned back toward the attentive crowd and gave a quiet smile.

"Good morning," she began firmly.  "Thank you for honoring us with your presence and your recognition . . . ."

* * *

'NOW!!'

The threads sang in ever more urgent harmony.  'Now!' they shouted in perfect chorus, 'or the moment is gone!'  Still she held back.

The rift between physical and ethereal bubbled and rolled, visible to all on the battlefield.  The pinpricks were scorching her now, peppering her skin with a searing heat.  If she waited any longer, her countless comrades in the ships above would be caught in the spell's devastation.

Inside the pocket of magic she'd worked, Kerri had created a perfect model of the planet Charth.  It hung suspended by time threads, a glittering ornament of creation.  So fragile, so vulnerable.  These people, the Charthinians, were her enemy, but must they all pay the price?  It was too much.

'Now,' the threads beseeched her one last time.  Finally Kerri obeyed their siren song.  Reaching into the void, she extended ice cold fingers and brushed the time strings away from the planet. But not all of them, as had been decided earlier, by her superiors. Instead, she brushed only those in her area, roughly one-fourth of the planet. She chose it because it was only fair that those who were to die should see their own executioner and that she should be with them if not among them.

\*\*\*

Kerri was talking to the audience, not paying any real attention to her speech. She'd given it several times before, these platitudes that had no purpose. To the veterans in the crowd—and there were many—no words were needed. To those who hadn't fought, no words could convey. She was merely offering a woefully inadequate bridge to span the immense gulf between protectors and protected. She had long since decided that the silent member behind her gave far greater testimony than she could.

She continued speaking, living more in the past and future than the present. The past held her captive, the price musers paid for using magic to harm. And the past held her future captive as well, for the silent assassin now walking the amphitheater's outside paths was coming to exact revenge on Kerri's deeds.

\*\*\*

Beyond the horizon came a deep groaning, as though the planet were mourning its own death. There were several hundred Charthinian and Imdlemonian solders on the field, all drawn to Kerri's spell as moths to flame. The wrenching agony of the wind snapped their thrall, however; and as a helpless flock, they turned toward their doom, which now surrounded them.

The blue skies of Charth darkened to deep purple as a blanket of magic coated it. Clouds vaporized in balls of flame as the spell—living pentrinsic code written on reality—settled toward the surface. Many ran helplessly and hopelessly away. Many others renewed their desperate attacks on Kerri, the author of their epitaphs. The rest merely waited for it, hoping only that it would be quick.

It was quick. The blanket—a slice of chaotic time that Kerri had impossibly given mass to—completed its purpose with horrific efficiency. First birds, then trees, then people and finally the ground itself exploded into dead matter as her covering of antireality snuffed out all life but hers. Nothing lived, above the ground, on it, or under it, for the blanket continued into the planet, shrinking with each passing moment until it finally reached the planet's molten core, where the spell finally ceased to exist. Horribly mutilated, the planet gave an agonized rumble and the blue skies returned. There was nothing left to witness it, save a single spark of life, forever marred by her unforgettable, unforgivable deed.

\* \* \*

Three minutes and the assassin would enter the amphitheater, raise his energy pistol and fire four times at Kerri. She'd easily dodge all four shots, then instinctively respond with a Vacuum Needle, crushing his insides into a useless pulp of blood and flesh. He'd not be the first to attempt killing her, nor the last.

But perhaps he didn't need to die. The wars were over. The soldiers had all carried the fiery burden for themselves and for others. Without looking at the wondrous strands of time and place that told their story so clearly to her, Kerri decided to act.

She abruptly stopped speaking and pressed her hands together, fingers splayed. All knew it was the opening of a Haven spell, the most common of magics worked in society. No one knew for whom it was designed.

Shifting gravity in the area surrounding her would-be assassin, Kerri flushed him out, causing him to stumble and lurch toward her. He desperately tried to bring his gun to bear; but she had suppressed it, making it impossible for energy to flow in the small pocket of reality his gun occupied. Seeing how completely he'd been exposed and disarmed, he nonetheless struggled as he continued approaching her against his will.

When he finally sank to his knees at the bottom of the stage, Kerri gently brushed her haven spell over him. Ruth stepped up, gun at the ready; but Kerri motioned her back.

"Let it go," she murmured to him quietly. "It's not worth it, to die for the dead."

"They're *my* dead!" he sobbed, still trying to activate his gun. "You killed them all! Don't you understand? You have to pay for what you've done."

"Don't *you* understand?" Kerri replied, her voice breaking. "I am paying. I'm paying for my actions, for the actions of your people and for the actions of my people." She swept a hand at the coffin. "That woman is paying, too. Every person who fought is paying. And they will pay while alive and long after they are dead. Until the last vestige of memory of them has passed, the dead pay. And you would add to the burden of your fallen? Of mine? Please, let it go."

The soft glow around him pulsed and quickened as the haven spell reached full potency. He cried, letting the gun fall soundlessly to the grass, then collapsing to his knees in agony and release.

\*\*\*

The pinpricks of the approaching ships were gone with the passing of the spell, replaced by the heavy throb of engines as an attack shuttle landed nearby. A pocket of antigravity pushed against her, and then ebbed. Inside the ship—and emanating from all the invasion fleet—were the overwhelming pulses of relief and joy, reinforced by the numbness of being witness to destruction unimaginable until today. The war was over, and the middle-aged woman with graying hair and sightless eyes standing on the dead surface of Charth was their heroine and their salvation and their burden.

Kerri's long battle was at last over. The throbbing died away. In her mind's eye, she saw the boarding ramp extending down.

But no one came out.

\*\*\*

"He might try again," Ruth commented as she guided their hov homeward. Behind them, Hinman was all abuzz over the day's events. The afternoon festivities and memorial rites had surged with extra energy, as though charged by the assassin's gun that had not been fired. The banquet of the evening was even more boisterous, as everyone—for the smallest moment—had been a part of the Six Planets War. Reliving or living for the first time, they had applauded Kerri's decision not to kill the assassin, as though her single action justified an entire war's worth of terrible deeds and merciless decisions.

"He may," Kerri replied, the cool of the evening air blowing through her hair as they slid over the glass road toward home. "He may even succeed. But whatever way he chooses, he's safe from me. I'll not hurt him ever."

"Certainly to defend yourself . . ."

"No. Not ever, Ruth. I've gave him his life today. It's no longer mine to take." She was quiet for a moment, gathering her thoughts. "I saw in him today the summation of all the war's emotions. I believe he showed me a reflection of the burden I carry. He was not my salvation, but perhaps he was a marker on the path."

She raised her head skyward and let the wind brush her face and tears. Tonight the nightmares would come, as they came every night for musers who used magic to harm others. But the nightmares would be more endurable for Kerri now. They were no longer her damnation.

"I'm tired," she whispered contentedly.

# MIND'S EYE INWARD

*October 11, 3014*

"Hello? May I help you?" Ruth's quiet, polite manner matched well with the dwelling, a modest-sized, yet well-kept farmhouse ten kilometers inland from the seaside town of Hinman, on the planet of Coda. There had come a knocking on the ancient yet perfectly proper front door of the home, and she was holding it partially open, appraising the woman who stood on the stoop.

"Yes. My name is Victoria Webber, and I represent the Application's Board for the Itinerant Teachers Association." She was a pleasantly plump woman in her forties, wearing the style of clothing that universally earmarked her as a competent administrator. She had green eyes set nicely into her full, auntish face, a thick head of curly, shoulder-length auburn hair that glimmered occasionally with blue and lilac light and a smile that was partly honest and partly confused. "I'm here to speak with General Kerri Marks," she added hesitantly.

"She prefers to be called Miss Marks these days, Miss Webber," Ruth corrected softly and opened the door wide. "The wars have been over for eight years now. Won't you come in, please? My name is Ruth Lu Chi and I'm Miss Marks' attendant. Call me Ruth."

"Thank you, Ruth." Victoria stepped in and was taken aback by the large size of the entryway. Though the house appeared to be little more than a cottage on the outside, the richly appointed hall and large forward sitting room showed the illusion. "My! How nice!" she exclaimed in genuine astonishment.

"Yes. The councils of all four planets awarded Miss Marks a substantial retirement fund at the conclusion of the wars, and Coda granted her this land and the home. We have worked quite hard to bring it to this state." Ruth indicated Victoria to follow her. They made their way through the main hall toward the open kitchen in the rear of the house.

"We?" Victoria asked politely. "I was not aware she required help to move around."

"Kerri?" Ruth replied in surprise. "I should say not! She's sixty-seven now, but looks and acts as a woman in her forties. I am her companion."

"To help her with her blindness?"

"I'm sorry, Miss Webber, but you misunderstand. I do not take care of her. I'm simply here as a friend. I was originally assigned to be her bodyguard since she'd acquired a number of enemies during the wars, but that was only a formality. Kerri is quite capable of taking care of herself. And me, if need be.

"I am her sounding board, her sympathetic ear, her conversationalist. She does not travel much these days, preferring to avoid what she calls the nonsensical claptrap that goes on when her identify is discovered. I keep the loneliness at bay."

To Victoria it looked as though she were about to say something more, but did not. They continued on in silence, their footfalls on the ceramic floor echoing pleasantly off the hard wood walls and glass surfaces. Everything went well together, Victoria decided, and that symentry put her at ease. Even Ruth, despite the younger woman's obvious extreme fitness and careful movements, seemed to go well with the relaxed atmosphere.

Kerri Marks was seated at her easel in the rear of the flower garden, the canvas turned from their sight. She was sitting motionless on a chair, studying the canvas, wearing a green and white dress that came up to her neck line. It neither billowed nor clung, nor did it seem neither too elegant nor too plain. Rather, it suited her frame and her location perfectly, making it seem as though she were the object of art and not the artist.

They walked silently toward her, and Victoria could see her more clearly. Of average build, she sat straight and proud, her shoulder back and her head up. Her skin remained smooth and white.

Whether from magics or just tender care, Victoria did not know; though knowing of the woman, she suspected the latter.   Her hair was not gray but silver. It was long, but done up neatly and exposed her neck. She seemed as proper and courtly as a porcelain doll. Yet this woman, whose cool blue eyes saw everything and nothing, had only ten years earlier single-handedly laid waste to a quarter of the surface of Charth. She seemed unaware of their presence.

"Kerri? Miss Victoria Webber has arrived. Shall I fix some tea?"

"Thank you, Ruth," she said crisply. "That would be very nice. And if you do not mind, I would like to speak to Mrs. Webber privately."

"Of course. I'll be back momentarily." Ruth gave Victoria a smile and returned to the kitchen.     "My apologies for not rising when you entered the garden, Mrs. Webber, but I wished to finish this before you arrived. What do you think?" She indicated the canvas.

Victoria stepped around to look at it and gasped. It was her, Victoria, as she looked when she was a small child—the eyes, the crooked smile, even the hands spread like a ballerina's as she showed off her favorite jumper. As she watched, the canvas rippled in color, and an invisible hand captured perfectly an image of her brother in the background.

"How . . . how . . . " she stammered.

"May I call you Victoria?" She did not wait for permission but continued. "I've been blind since I was eighteen, Victoria, and have used my mind's eye for nearly fifty years. Trained and used enough, it is possible for the mind's eye to see reality for what it is."

"And what is it, Miss Marks?" she asked, stunned at the realness of the painting.

"I'll call you Victoria, you'll call me Kerri," she ordered gently. "Reality is the physical wrapped around the ephemeral and bonded by the temporal."

"The Marks Refinement of the Woldheim Principle of Spectral Reality?"

"You know it then?" Kerri asked in a pleased voice, her smile lighting up both her face and the flower garden.

"A little," Victoria admitted. "I only know it from my senior year, and I brushed up on it before coming here. It states that the temporal and physical can be identified and modified. The ephemeral is unalterable by outside force, but changes gradually according to the soul's awareness of reality. That's why you called me Mrs. Webber."

"That's correct. I can hear reality as it cloaks you and am able to understand the harmonies. Your soul sings of a deep love that can only come from marriage, with the throbbing undertones of satisfaction that . . . ." Victoria flushed. Kerri broke off and gave a small chuckle that made the canvas quiver. "Forgive me, Victoria. That's far too personal. Here, please accept this portrait as a gift."

"Thank you very much, Miss . . . ." At the woman's gently reproving look, she caught herself. "I mean, Kerri. But that would be inappropriate and may be construed as . . ."

"A bribe?" Kerri interrupted incredulously, then laughed. "I should hardly think so. I'm aware enough of my own position to know I can have anything I wish. For me, bribes are utterly unnecessary. But I am determined to do things the correct way. Besides, I already know you've turned down my request to be reinstated as an itinerant teacher. The Board has turned me down, rather. So a bribe would be useless."

"How did you know? Or did you?"

"Oh, I knew. If I can hear your most private realities, I can certainly hear the songs of your minor irritations, woman. Come. The art is yours as a gift for having the guts to tell me to my face. I'll have it sent to your home. Now," she patted a bench beside her, "have a seat and tell me why I'm unfit to teach children."

They chatted for thirty minutes, bantering back and forth over Kerri's qualifications, shortcomings and risks. Ruth, according to her friend's wishes, left them alone after serving tea, keeping an eye on them from the kitchen. Ruth herself was of the Chin race, her ancestors having come from a single province on Earth centuries earlier. She was a woman in her mid-thirties, of handsome beauty, with yellowish brown skin, lean frame and strong shoulders. Her black hair was short and thick. Her almond eyes were so black, Kerri had often commented, that they gave Ruth's entire form a deep glow of earthen peace. It was Kerri's thorough understanding of Ruth and her willingness to let Ruth into her world that had forged their friendship. There was no physically intimate or romantic relationship between them of course. But there were times when it seemed as though they were married, such was their trust and fondness for each other.

She looked out over the scene, seeing both the beauty of the garden and the best locations for ambush and attack. Kerri could easily hold off multiple attacks on multiple planes, and Victoria Webber was not nor would ever be a threat. For Ruth, however, the habits died hard, and she maintained a careful watch, conscious of the nearby phased fusion pistol she could have in her hand and firing in less than two seconds.

But nothing more distressing than Victoria's obvious discomfort at facing a formidable and iron-willed Kerri occurred, and the talk came to an otherwise pleasant conclusion. Ruth caught the slight nod from Kerri and heard the gentle singing in her mind and escorted Victoria to the door.

"How did it go?" Ruth asked as they walked through the hallway. It was only an hour until sunset, and the temperature was a refreshing twenty degrees, so the roof had been turned off to allow the stars to shine down into the home.

"Not well," Victoria said honestly. In just the short time she'd been with them, she'd come to like both women. "I personally feel that though she is something of a risk because of her past as an attack muser, the risk is very small and is far outweighed by the positive impact she could have as a children's teacher. The Board did not see it that way, however."

"The Board is right," Ruth said bluntly. At Victoria's shocked look, Ruth shook her head. "Again I think you misunderstand me, Mrs. Webber. I love Kerri very much. She's my sister and my mother and my best friend all at once. And she truly does wish to be a teacher again. I think that had the wars not happened, Kerri would have been one of the best teachers ever. I know that had I any children I would have been honored to have her teach them.

"The wars did happen, though, and the toll on Kerri was appalling. You know, of course, that she taught musers how to use attack spells?" Ruth asked.

Victoria nodded.

Ruth continued, "Did you also know that of the eight hundred and twenty-one that she taught, only one hundred and four survived the war?"

"Why?" Victoria asked. They'd come to the front door, but neither seemed aware of it.

"Because attack musers were the main reason we won the war, Victoria. They were targeted constantly during the entire fifty-one years of the war. So because of Kerri, we won and the Imdlemodin dictatorship with its annihilatory practices was destroyed. But because of what Kerri taught, over seven hundred of her students were killed. And now she wants to teach again?" Ruth shook her head firmly. "To do so invites disaster. No. Despite her wishes, this is the best way, and I think she knows it."

"Then why did she try so hard to get reinstated?"

"Because a small part of her was hoping the ITA would have come to a different conclusion. She was clinging to the dream of erasing the wars and what they did to her, so she could take the path meant for her. That she could make a gentle impact on her planets and peoples, not the horribly brutal one she did."

"But she saved us," Victoria protested. "Without her, there would be no ITA, no children, no people. Not on our planets at least. She did more for us in the wars than she could do in a lifetime of teaching."

Ruth smiled at her and at her innocence of the cost of war. "That brings little comfort, Victoria, when the ghosts of those you've killed come to you in your nightmares." She reached out with her left hand and squeezed Victoria's shoulder. "Thank you for showing proper respect by coming here personally to speak to Kerri. Good afternoon."

***

"They said no," Kerri commented as Ruth sat beside her in the garden. She'd brought out a bottle of wine and a tray of cheese, bread and fruit for their evening meal. It sat between them on a small table, adding a perfect caress to the gathering twilight's ambiance.

"Yes, I know. Victoria told me. She was disappointed with their decision."

"You weren't."

"No." Ruth said nothing more. Instead she poured more chilled white wine into two long glasses. They ate quietly for several minutes, absorbing the sounds and scents of a Codan summer evening. Overhead, in the impossibly crystal skies, hundreds of stars were twinkling, seeming to draw extra energy from the white sun that was just dipping below Burial Ridge to the west.

"In all honesty, Ruth," Kerri sighed. "I was hoping to be denied reinstatement, too. As much as I want to teach, I'm much more afraid. Afraid of myself and afraid for the children."

"You didn't want them to see the monster you've become," Ruth said, causing Kerri to flinch. "You didn't want them to begin to idolize you and to want to be like you."

"The proper role model means so much, Ruth." Kerri reached out with a trembling hand and picked up a slice of apple and cheese. "Mine was my teacher when I was only six years old."

"Deborah Hennessy."

"Yes. I still see her at night, before the nightmares come. She was so happy, so full of life, and so very interested in seeing her children grow up. Oh, how dearly I wanted to be like her!" She took an uncharacteristically quick swallow of wine. "What would happen, I wonder, if I felt the look of a young girl into my eyes and want to be like me? What would I say to her?"

"Do it, Kerri," Ruth said simply.

"What?" Kerri's eyes blinked back tears. "What do you mean?"

"You know exactly what I mean. I know you can, and it's your fondest wish to teach again. I promise you I'll do everything I can to support you. I promise from the bottom of my heart. But it's you who has to take the first step."

"Thank you, love. It is so reassuring to know I would always have you at my side. But it wouldn't be right. I should not improperly use . . . . "

"Improperly use!" Ruth snapped back, angry at her friend's misplaced sense of propriety. "You can save millions of lives and end a war by reducing fifty million square kilometers of a planet to carbonized ooze, but you can't . . . oh!" She abruptly stood up. "This isn't about what is owed to you, Kerri. This about what you still owe to us. Think of it that way. Turn your mind's eye inward, and you'll see my point."

Ruth gathered up the remains of their dinner. Holding the cutting board in one hand, she laid the other on Kerri's still firm shoulder.

"It will cost you everything, Kerri, but sometimes even the highest price can be easy to pay. Good night."

Kerri felt Ruth walking back into the house. Looking after her dear friend with her mind's eye, she could see the lovely woman even better than Ruth could see herself. Her radiant blue determination of caring burned as brilliantly as Kerri's own stubbornness. But should she be stubborn in this? Could Ruth be right?

Later, as she prepared for bed, Kerri continued to think about it. Her room was across from Ruth's and was a short call away, but both women tended to leave the other alone at night, except when Kerri's nightmares became too strong.

Moving silently and carefully, Kerri pulled out the next morning's change of clothing and laid them out precisely on the couch at the foot of her bed. Her bedroom had no lights of course. Kerri preferred shutting off her mind's eye at night. Her nightmares seem to ease if she removed herself entirely from her magical perceptions, so all was dark.

She turned down the bed covers, then hesitated. Going back to her heavy wooden dresser, she opened the bottom drawer and pulled out a second set of night clothing, holding it against her cheek.

A young girl's nightgown—Ruth had bought it for her several years earlier, knowing the pull she still felt for teaching. It was an ankle-length nightshirt, made of flannel, with lace along the neck and cuffs. Ruth had told her it was light yellow and bespeckled with bright white suns. There was a matching set of panties and night socks, perfect for keeping a little girl warm and safe on even the coldest snowy night.

Stroking the material that was meant to protect a child's innocence and nature as well as her small body, Kerri felt a soft melancholy sweep over her. She was glad that ITA had turned her down. And despite Ruth's assurances and encouragement, Kerri was determined to allow the chance to pass a final time. Her place was here, in this house, quietly removed from the public that so admired and so feared her.

Feeling better, she laid the nightgown, panties and socks on the couch, to be put away in the morning, and retired to bed. Somehow, she knew the nightmares would not be as cruel to her tonight.

\*\*\*

Ruth awoke suddenly, the old training resurfaced. She froze in place to avoid detection, to determine the source of the attack. Realization of her surroundings came and she relaxed. In the comfortable dark of her room, she raised up on her arms to discover what had woken her.

Looking around, she saw that the darkness had a decidedly green tint to it and that the air was painted ever so lightly with vanilla. Worried for Kerri, she arose and pulled on her robe, then went to check on her friend.

Kerri was still in bed, but the room itself was glowing and gently throbbing with magical light, coming from nowhere and everywhere at once. She heard the laughter of water over rocks and smelled wildflowers. Her eyes teared and blinked rapidly from the brilliant white sunlight that she could not see but nonetheless felt on her face. She looked again at Kerri. She was sleeping peacefully, unmolested by the nightmares. Not wishing to disturb the haven spell nor the old woman's rest, Ruth returned to bed and soon drifted off to sleep.

\* \* \*

It was morning when Ruth next awoke. She sat up in bed, stretched and let out a loud, most unladylike yawn. From below the foot of her bed, she heard a childish giggle.

"Hello?" she called in a quiet voice, rubbing her eyes. "Who's down there?"

There came another giggle, and Ruth saw the top of a small head. It was covered with brown hair done up into a rough, floppy ponytail and tied back by small hands. As Ruth watched in wonderment at the little intruder, the head moved slowly around the bed and up along the side, keeping low, as if to make a surprise attack.

And an attack it turned out to be.

"Surprise!" shrieked the girl with a laugh, suddenly jumping up and launching herself onto Ruth.

"Oof!" Ruth gasped, her hands shooting out to pry the knee out of her stomach. The girl was only about six years old, with brown hair and cool blue eyes. She wore a yellow flannel nightgown with white suns on it and a matching set of socks. The suns were bright, but not as bright as the girl's face, which shown with unbound joy and love of life, unburdened by demons, ghosts or memories of deeds best forgotten. She was smiling at Ruth now, a beautiful, unreserved smile that proudly sported a space the grownup tooth had not yet begun to fill.

"Gotcha, Ruth!" she shouted happily, squirming all over the woman, yanking back the covers and plopping down on her again. "Come on! Let's get up and go to town! I know!" she gasped with a sudden idea. "We can get some hot chocolate and sweet rolls at the market an' walk to the beach, an' get our feet wet, okay?" She looked at Ruth with hope and complete trust in her eyes.

"I—I suppose we could . . . could do that," Ruth stammered out, trying as hard as possible to adjust to the impossible. She looked down at the girl as she nestled in the crook of her arm, staring up at Ruth with a suddenly serious look as the blue eyes studied her closely.

"You promised you'd take care of me," she stated solemnly.

Ruth felt her heart burst open with joy, and she wept, pressing the girl tight against her.

"I did promise you that, Kerri," she said with both happiness and tears. "And I always keep my promises. I'll be here always, helping you grow up into a lovely young woman."

"Oh! Thank you, Ruth!" she laughed and hugged her mightily, her little arms tight against Ruth's neck. She suddenly pushed off and looked her in the eye.

"I'm gonna be a teacher when I grow up," she declared with the unwavering certainty of youth. "I really, really am."

\*\*\*

AUTHOR'S NOTE

Here ends the first part of Kerri Marks' adventures. She did grow up into a lovely woman, her friend and mother Ruth Lu Chi constantly at her side. She also retained all her natural magical abilities, though she did need to relearn how to use them.

Kerri was eventually discovered by the enemies she'd made in the Six Planets Wars, and became a hunted fugitive. No longer having the aggressive powers she'd developed during the wars, she and others like her were forced to flee to three, small, uninhabited planets in the Centaur system, located in a distant sector of the galaxy. Their society—based on magic more than technology—ultimately became the source of the most powerful musers ever known in history.

But that is another . . .

. . . or two.

# MOVING DAY

*Earth Date: September 18, 3038*

He packed everything, giving one last glance at the reason he was leaving. How such a small object could cause so great a change in so many lives only demonstrated the irony of man's struggle for control in a universe that always enjoyed a good joke. As if to redeliver the sick punch line, the device gave a quick chirp and winked its blue eye.

The hallway was empty of people, but filled with tension. Eric walked its length to the eledisc, his three suitcases tagging along, playfully banging into each other in a contest to see which would be first. The ghost doors were all set to private—the planed energy showing a silent white surface. Eric knew his neighbors—using the term loosely—were staring at him through the one-way shimmers, glad he was finally going.

Ah! to be different! Eric gave a disgusted shake of the head as he stepped on the eledisc. It dropped him quietly the sixteen floors to the building exit. He'd always known he was different, from the time he understood his own existence around nine months of age. His parents had discovered that difference shortly thereafter at his second birthday when he used his birthday present, a new writing tabinal, to trisect an angle using, until that moment, an undiscovered, theorem derived from the planed intersection of two asymmetric cones and an inverted sphere.

The eledisc dinged arrival at ground, and Eric stepped off, his luggage following. The medium suitcase had established dominance and was at Eric's heels, leading the other two, much like three eager school students, anxious to please the teacher.

School. He had started very young. His gift with mathematics sent him shooting through the levels. Eric attended Coda University at Hinman by his tenth birthday. He tutored at eleven and taught at fourteen. Now, at twenty-six, Eric was a respected professor, known all over Coda and numerous other planets as the man who could count to *i*, the square root of negative one. That he was different was an understatement.

The shuttle appeared on the other side of the common and floated quietly on its scheduled stops, circling the common toward him. The eledisc pinged again, and Eric turned, already knowing who he'd see.

Jamie, of course. She was different, too. Exactly different. Unlike Eric, however, Jamie was far more chipper. She was twenty-four and had a life not unlike his. She was also a professor at CUH, teaching the intricacies of programming with pentrinsic code exclusively in spectral reality, a frustrating hobble to say the least.

She flashed him a big smile; and as always, Eric was unable to resist smiling back.

"Good morning, Jamie," he sighed, struggling to lose his smile. Her dark eyes lit up even more. Her long blond hair seemed to shimmer with happiness in the early morning sea breeze. "I take it you received the same gift last night, compliments of Codan Internal Affairs?"

"Uh-huh." She whistled softly to her single suitcase. It yipped once and crowded close to her. She pouted at Eric's demeanor.

"Why so glum, chum?" she asked. "It's not the end of the world."

"It is for us," he replied, "at least, the end of this one."

"Nah," she said, dismissing the situation with a wave. "We both knew this was coming, Eric. Coda held out the longest in the System of Planets, but even they had to give in sooner or later. And the CIA is being really reasonable about it."

"I suppose," he grudgingly admitted. "But that doesn't change the fact that we're being declared *persona non grata* on our native planet. Being nice about it doesn't make it right."

"C'mon, Eric," Jamie said reasonably. "You know that all the normal humans have been watching us for over thirty years now. And while they don't have any real reason to fear us, in their limited perceptions they can't know that for sure."

"We've told them over and over," he countered, then gave up on the old, useless defense and changed the subject. "Did you hear about Hans?"

"Professor Fÿrgrun? At Ball Chasers U? No."

"In the middle of night, Deerkin Race Authority broke into his home and attached that damned tracker to him against his will. And the DRA has been marking our kind for years."

Jamie said nothing.

"What's to stop something like that from happening to us, Jamie? Or to others like us?"

"Eric," she said quietly, "that won't happen to us and you know it. I'm sorry about Hans, but BCU is on Deerkin, and Coda is not Deerkin." She shuddered and hugged herself. "Sometimes I think we humans have advanced too fast for our own good." She looked away, then back, smiling again.

"Besides, Eric, Hans is quite capable of writing a Remove program and plucking that thing right off his temple."

"That's not the point, Jamie!" Eric said. "It's the fact that he even has to . . . . " he broke off as Jamie stood on tiptoe and kissed him on the cheek.

"Cheer up, Eric! We've got an adventure in front of us! We leave our lives behind and start new ones today! C'mon, admit it. You're kind of excited about all of us being together, away from the stares, away from the nervous smiles, away from the innuendo."

"Yeah, I'm excited," Eric grumped. Darn her! he thought. She *always* makes me smile.

"Okay, okay," he admitted, smiling. "You've ruined my grouchy mood. I am looking forward to it. The limitations the University were putting on me chaffed. I understand that normal humans can't comprehend ireality theorems and proofs, let alone visualize them; but I still hated restricting myself to spectral reality," he said, using the human term for spectral reality. "It's such a confining area of study."

"Me, too," Jamie agreed. "Shifting pentrinsic code from its native environment to force it into a spectral reality-only platform has been giving me headaches. Now I'll have students who can see pentrinsic come to life as it weaves between the two realities as it ought." She sighed. "And believe me, Eric! Teaching ten-year-olds will be a whole bunch more fun than instructing twenty and thirty-year-olds."

The shuttle floated to them and stopped. The shimmering air beneath it shrank as the driver lowered the bus a meter for easy access. The door opened.

Jamie grabbed Eric's hand and tugged.

"Hey, Eric," she suggested playfully, "let's leave in style!" She looked off into the middle distance. Eric could sense her writing the program. Seventeen fives, forty-one threes, nineteen twos, seven ones and a single zero.

Jamie's feet lifted off the ground as the Fly program took hold. She kept tugging him, laughing.

"Nonstop to the space port!" she laughed, "now departing!"

Eric chuckled, finally giving in completely to her persistent joy. He quickly coded the Fly spell and soared up with her. They ascended to a hundred meters and made for the port, some thirty kilometers to the south. People poured out of the shuttle to point and watch.

"Don't forget our stuff!" she shouted at him, "or no tip!"

"Yes'm!" he laughed back, and cast a Come Along spell on the luggage.

# *Jenny*

Earth date: April 3, 3049
Centaur date: Marks Matrix: 15th Remembrance, Tier 4*i*, 395th Vibration of Chronostring 1093; 3violet2 R shading. (2nd reality expression, simplified for linear cohesion and *Homo sapiens* comprehension.)

Jennifer Navarra was flying.

Far, far beneath her was her home town of Hennessey, the only town on the newly settled planet of Centaur's Heart. It looked like an exquisite toy, sparkling with lights from the houses as the people woke up to start another day. Wanting to see as much as possible before waking up, Jenny swooped down further, looking for her friend Nick's home. She found it, the ceiling opaque in the early morning light, and floated close beside his window. He didn't have on the room's dream shade, but she didn't take advantage. They were best friends so he respected her privacy, too.

She could see just inside his window, though, and onto his puter desk. Magic didn't work in the puterverse; and as she was inside a dream, Jenny could see the puter desk as only a fuzzy sound that smelled like warm blue. What did stand out on the desk, in pulsing splendor, was Nick's sposedto. Identical to hers, it was what had made them friends to begin with, when each discovered the other's sposedto while on an astral field trip to the Crab Nebula. He thought hers was too tomboyish, while she'd thought his too girly, especially for a nine-year-old boy. It didn't take long for each of them to stick their tongues out at each other and start name-calling. From there a friendship had started. Now, almost a year later . . .

"Jennifer."

Jenny looked around and saw way up in the sky the soft pink and yellow of her mother's Shifting spell gently calling to her to wake up. She took one last look at Nick's window and flew up into the sky, moving out of her dream and shifting into the real world of school, play and magic.

She opened her eyes, immediately awake, and jumped out of her top bunk bed, her head accidentally bumping the Shifting spell sphere and scattering it into a shower of gentle sparks that followed her to the floor. She landed on the carpet. Careful not to waken her three-year-old sister Alyeta, Jenny pulled a change of clothes out of her dresser and closet and raced off to get ready for another day. Another day with Nick.***

"My!" her mother laughed as Jenny ran down the stairs and into the kitchen. "That was fast! Did you wake your sister?"

"No," Jenny said, shaking her head while reaching for an orange from the kitchen's tree. The weather on Centaur's Heart being as perfect as it was, along with its new inhabitants being the kind of people they were, kitchens were outside the home. Theirs was a largish yard of rich earth that grew fruits, vegetables, herbs, shelter and furniture.

"Do you have your sposedto?" her mother asked, unable to resist the motherly reminding urges, yet she knew her daughter never went anywhere without it.

"Moooooommmm," Jenny said, rolling her pitch black eyes, their cobalt blue flecks dancing with disguised cheerfulness. Her mother's eyes were also dark, but Jenny was second generation Marks, so her race attributes had no trace of *homo Sapiens* in them. "I'm ten years old! It's not like I'm gonna forget *that*." Nonetheless, she patted her skirt pocket and checked. The sposedto hummed back in vanilla and tufted greenfinch, Jenny's favorite sensations.

"All right, then," her mother replied, smiling and kissing her on top of the head. "You'd best hurry off to class. Your father will stop by later this afternoon and walk you home, okay?"

"Okay." Retrieving the sposedto, Jenny whispered to it. "'Member, I'm s'posed to walk home with Dad today." Jenny knew she was old enough to walk home by herself, but there was just no way she would give up walking home with her dad. She shoved the sposedto back in its home and waved to her mother. "Bye, Mom!"

Jenny ran through the house and out the front ghost door, making it bubble and snap as her aura clashed ever so slightly with the energy plane of the door. Magic and technology could exist together—magic nothing more than incomprehensible and imaginary technology—but their physical laws always vied for superiority. The result was an uneasiness in spectral reality whenever they bumped.

Outside, it was a brilliant day. Centaur, the star around which the three planets of Heart, Hoof and Soul raced in the same orbit, was very similar to her parents' distant home planet of Coda, so small and intensely white. The skies were similar too in that they were vivid blue and crystal clear, allowing the Centaur's Mane—the asteroid belt in orbit fifty million kilometers further out—to sparkle and paint the sky all twenty and one-half hours of the day.

The breeze was fresh, chilled and soft. Jenny started conjuring her Feather spell; then she remembered her mother wanted her to get more exercise. She wrinkled her face briefly, but obeyed, deciding to walk to school instead. It would take her an extra twenty minutes this way, but at least she could scrounge for the wild strawberries that hid in the brambles on the town's outskirts. S he tied back her waist-length blonde hair so it wouldn't catch in the prickers and hurried off across the Common.

The strawberries were tucked off the path a meter or so. The police determined that Jenny had found some, but didn't have time to eat any before she'd been taken.

*** 

Nick lay in his bed, staring up through the clear ceiling and into the glittering Mane. The belt wavered and shimmered more these past three nights, now that he cried himself to sleep. Poor Jenny! He didn't know where she was, but his imagination could easily create many horrible places. So young and sheltered—the awfulness of being taken from parents and friends provided wild and uncontrollable paths to the darker corners of his mind.

Downstairs, the police were again sitting with his parents, comforting them and quietly helping them remember and relive anything in the past few weeks that may give a clue as to what had happened to her. Reconstruction magics were not aggressive—they harm the caster as much as the target—but neither were they beneficial spells, so there was a toll exacted on all in the casting area. To avoid too much harsh magic, Nick had been sent up early.

The now familiar blue aura glimmered and pressed against his energy door, causing it to chirp and cascade. Grateful for any distraction, he rolled on his side and watched the struggle between physical and imaginary technology. The real and unreal playfully tugged and pulled at each other, neither interested in winning but both intent on competing.

At least, that's how Nick saw it. He knew there was much more to the relationship between the two, but Reticulated Physics covered that and he didn't start that until he was eleven. Still, Nick knew enough about Inserted Realities Theory to understand that the constant pressure between the two kept a colorful and vibrant balance; neither letting the other work within, yet both . . .

Nick's deep black eyes suddenly opened wide, the blue flecks in them matching the blue of the door perfectly. The patterns in the door were suddenly so clear! Now he knew why. Hurriedly, he jumped out of bed and dressed into his shorts and shirt. Snatching up his "carry everywhere" stuff of sposedto, gum, jackknife, lightline, foot anchor and credid card, he ran to his desk. The puterverse link was active, so he brushed it closed and opened the window. The dream shield was on all the time now—a precaution nearly everyone in town was observing—so he canceled it. Such was his excitement that his trembling fingers tugged the wrong plenary strings twice before he finally stroked the off-magenta one that dropped the shield. He waved his hands in front of him, wiping closed the spatial rift he'd opened to cast the spell; then clambered out the window. It was a ten-meter fall to the ground, but by simply diverting the gravity skyward with a Little G spell, it seemed only ten centimeters. A gentle shifting and an insertion of 2 fives, 17 threes, a single one and 13 zeros quickly raised the Dream Shield behind him.

"I'm coming, Jenny," he said quietly to himself, casting Flight and going skyward. He reached a height of one-hundred meters. He then angled his direction toward the brambles where his best friend in all the worlds had last been.

\*\*\*

Vince Feggault tapped out the eight-digit code, and the door viewer depolarized to allow him to see in. The girl couldn't see out, but it didn't matter: she was so tamed by the constant accessing in the puterverse that she couldn't see anything and didn't care.

Nor could she feel anything. Not the ultraviolet intravenous system that fed her. Not the chin and body straps that kept her strapped to the gravity chair. Not even the harsh redness on her neck. To Vin, it looked infected. He didn't know whether Cheats got sick easily or not. They didn't seem to, but maybe they healed themselves all the time. That must be it, he decided. Low power laze guns rarely caused infection.

She'd been lazed and knocked out as she crawled through the bushes, reaching for that biggest, tastiest strawberry. Vin and Hutchins had been on Centaur's Heart for five days. This was the first chance they'd had to snatch a kid—they all seemed to freakin' fly everywhere. They had only the one chance, but they made it count. A quick shot, an unconscious kid and a hasty retreat to their docked ship. Ten minutes after Hutchins pulled the trigger of the gun, he was pressing the ignition switch for the fusion engines. They cleared the Mane thirty hours later and engaged the ball to maximum for the ship: 20000 FTL. Now sixty hours out, the Centaur system was seventy light years behind them, with nearly 6500 light years to go. Four long months with only Hutchins and an oblivious Cheat for company.

Shaking his head in pity at the sight of the numbed and helpless girl, Vin released the view switch, and the port went opaque.

"How's our ten million cred cargo doin'?" Hutchins asked from the pilot's chair when Vin had made his way forward.

"Not so hot," he said. "She's got an infection from the laze, and I don't think she's moved since we accessed her." He paused, not wanting to sound too sympathetic. "Don'cha think we oughta ease the access down a level or two, Hutch?"

"Yeah, right," Hutchins snorted in reply. "We let her get free of that field for even a minute and we're cooked, Vin. Those thought police on that weirdo planet will have her aura or brain waves or some crap pinned down inna sec and we're toast."

"At seventy light years?" He shook his head. "They can't be that powerful."

"Believe it, Vin," Hutchins replied. "You heard what we were told when we took on this job."

"But she's harmless, Hutch," Vin countered. "Look, I ain't no saint, but the kid's gotta be in good condition for us to get paid. Them Terrans need to find out why magic don't work on Earth, and they gotta experiment on a healthy Cheat." Vinny leaned over the chair and looked at Hutchins, "I got bills to pay, Hutch, an' I need all my cut."

"She'll be fine," Hutchins snapped. "Sure, them Cheat kids got weak bodies, but their minds are tough. And if you think I'm gonna give her even half a chance to use that magic, then you're weak. In the head."      Vin mumbled but relented. Hutchins was a good part-ner—a little abrasive but with a clear head and a solid honest streak. Honesty was an important trait to have in this kind of business.

* * *

It was a brittle surface Jenny was standing on. Moving too fast seemed to shatter the ground and send painful slivers through her soul. Deep, deep down she knew she'd been accessed into the puterverse, but her mind cried out that this was a nightmare. She tried the few sleep spells that she knew—Shift, AlterDreamscape, Invita-tion—but none worked. If anything, they intensified the depression in the electron air and made more brittle the ground that terrified her.

What's happened to me? she thought despairingly. Where were mom and dad? How long have I been here? Ireality didn't glow in the puterverse, so there was no way to tell the time from color hues. One day? Two? A week?

There came a sudden tingling in her body and she jumped, fearful of another painful shattering. Nothing happened, so Jenny allowed herself to cautiously turn in a slow circle and inspect her puterverse prison.

Again, she saw nothing save the brittle, thorny surface she was standing on and the endless black sky of the puterverse. Sighing with a voice that sounded like wind through tall, wet grass, Jenny sat down carefully, the only other position she was allowed, since lying down cracked the surface.

The tingling started again, and this time Jenny was able to locate it. It was *on* her. Scared, she began running over her puterverse form. Her body was a blend of fiery pink with occasional flashes of butternut. She wore no clothes in the puterverse, but she wasn't naked, since all forms are only general. Her long blonde hair flowed easily enough but was the same color as the rest of her.

The tingling continued and Jenny was finally able to locate the source. It was just off her left leg, below her waist but above her knee. Curious fingers probed at the invisible object, feeling out its shape. It was small and round. . . her sposedto!

With fumbling fingers she worked the ball into her hand and she squeezed it.

"'Member, I'm s'posed to walk home with Dad today."

It was her s'posed from the last normal morning she had. But why would it go off now? And in the puterverse?

She started to return it to the invisible pocket when it went off again.

"'Mem . . . I . . . Home . . . Today."

That was strange. Was her sposedto damaged?

"Home. Home."

Her eyes widened with sudden hope.

"Home. Home today."

Nick! It had to be Nick! Somehow, he was manipulating her sposedto. Her emotions soared! He was going to save her! But he needed to tell her more. What if she made another s'posed? Tentatively, she put the device close to her mouth.

"I'm s'posed to make sure Nick knows where I am right now."

She no sooner spoke than her lips, lower face and hand went numb. Excited, she moved the sposedto away from her face. Now only her hand was numb. Of course! Nick was using magic to interface with a binary peripheral device into a trinary reality. Magic was in reality pentrinsic code; a code consisting of zeroes, ones, twos, threes and fives used to program reality. It didn't work in the puterverse's trinary reality, but a binary device could be manipulated by either pentrinsic or unbound trinary code. And a sposedto was a binary device.

She quickly thought over her past year's math lessons. Her race, *homo Magicus*, were born with innate math skills far outstripping even their most learned *homo Sapiens* cousins. Counting to $i$, the square root of negative one, was child's play to a *homo Magicus* person, the first lesson taught in kindergarten. Jenny and her race lived simultaneously in spectral reality and ireality, which was the reason for her generation's physical attributes.

According to the Marks Refinement of the Woldheim Principle of Spectral Reality, reality is the physical wrapped around the ephemeral and bonded by the temporal. The twelfth itemporal regenerated theorem of the Marks Refined Principle stated that because the puterverse was a trinary reality, which combined all three spectral dimensions onto a single plane which was referenced by the temporal plane, it was possible to insert a focused line of ireality into trinary reality. But since the insertion relied on an unlinked temporal line, it quickly collapsed to a point. That was why magic didn't work in the puterverse; there was no way to anchor a point in trinary reality, since a point contains no dimension beyond temporal. The theorem stated that pentrinsic could survive in a trinary existence, but that its existence was limited to a point in time, which was no time.

But Nick must have realized he could use a dual fixed anchor—spectral reality itself—to act as a line of communication between pentrinsic and trinary. Their sposedtos!

"Make . . . Sure . . . Make sure."

Nick was communicating with her! And if Jenny had any doubts, the next words were proof positive.

"Nick know now . . . Home today. . . Nick tell now . . . I make sure home today." The sposedto beeped and turned off.

Jenny waited until sensation returned to her hand, then carefully put her sposedto back. The battery might have died. She'd forgotten to New Life the charge, and it had been on this whole time while accessed in the puterverse. She wondered how long she had to wait. It didn't matter! Nick was going to rescue her! How romantic!

*  *  *

Exhausted, Nick shut off his sposedto and picked it up from the shrubs. He canceled the Been There spell he'd cast to highlight the spot Jenny had last been. The soft glow faded from the ground, leaving it dark.

Nick stood up carefully on very wobbly feet. He'd never been so drained! It was like he'd been running and running and running. Magic never tired any Marks; his exhaustion came from forcing his coding into a reality other than spectral.

Fortunately, he was back in spectral and ireality, so casting was effortless again. He cast Flight and made his way home, staying close to the ground just in case.

Nick knew he'd be in trouble for leaving his room, but he didn't care. He had to rescue Jenny!

*  *  *

Hutchins swore, once and with extreme vileness. Vin jerked from his nap, partially from Hutchins outburst and partly because the ship began vibrating badly.

"Wha . . . What's wrong?"

"I don't know!" He barked back. He kept glancing over the controls. "Everything's fine, only it's not! We're dropping speed! Down to 15000 FTL!" He swung hard eyes tinged with just a trace of fear on Vin. "I think we've been caught, Vin."

Vin swore as well and ran to check on their prisoner.

She was unchanged after four days.

"She's still out, Hutch," Vin said over the comlink. "No way she could have sent a message or done any cheating."

"How can you know, Vin? We're from Earth. We've never seen Cheats before."

"But they said . . . ."

"Yeah," came the bitter reply, "but they ain't here. It's our asses, Vin." The comm went silent, and Vin thought Hutch had signed off.

"Hutch?" Vin said tentatively. Both were hardened men of ruthless character with brutal backgrounds, but magic was far beyond their experience.

"I'm thinkin'!" He swore again. "We're about to go sublight, Vin. This is gonna get nasty." Another pause. "All right, let's play our hole card. Wake her up and bring her here. But do it quick, before she can react."

"What're you doin', Hutch?" Vin whispered as he shut off the comm. Hesitantly, he pressed his hand on the door release. The door went transparent; then shut off, giving Vin access to the stupefied girl.

* * *

The platform shattered abruptly. Jenny screamed in surprise, but then realized there was no pain this time. Something different was happening.

"C'mon, kid," came a grumpy, rough voice.

Jenny blinked her eyes, feeling sick to her stomach and itchy all over. Her neck hurt.

"Let's go." A big hand clamped on her arm and led her. She stumbled behind him, trying to help him help her. Even if this man was mean and had stolen her from her home, it was her nature to be of service to everyone.

"Where . . . are . . . " she started to mumble, but was cut off.

"Shut it. We're in a tight spot, which means you're in a tighter one."

"Huh?" she asked halfheartedly, her mind only now beginning to adjust. Another man had spoken. She'd never heard accents like theirs before. They crackled with sharpness and brittle anger.

"Listen close," the second voice was saying. Through blurry vision, Jenny could just make him out. "Your people are coming to get you. Only they aren't going to get you. You'll never see your planet or friends again. Understand?"

She shook her head, fear pouring over her.

"You can't!" she said in a quiet voice. "It's not right! Please! Let me go! I want my mom and dad!"

"Shut up!" he snapped. "If they get you, then that means they got us. And there's no way Vin and I are . . ." He broke off suddenly as the ship stopped vibrating and began shaking. "What's going on?"

"Hutch! They're hailing us on the comlink!"

"Fine. Let me handle it. C'mere, kid."

"My name's Jennifer. Jennifer Navarra. How can I help?"

"Kid, I don't care if your name's Roids Cavanaugh. You wanna help? Stay quiet, don't pull no tricks, and bleed when I cut you."

Terrified, Jenny nodded her head and folded her hands at her waist, just as her parents had taught her. There were the first non-Marks people she'd ever seen, and she was determined to be of service. Even if that meant bleeding when cut.

"Terran ship *Blue Scout*, this is Centaur Space Control. Please respond."

"Ignore it!" Vin said.

"Please do not ignore us, *Blue Scout*. We know you have Jennifer Navarra with you, and we are requesting her safe return."

Hutch stared at the link. The ship continued to shake, its vibrations increasing dramatically, and there came an ominous creaking from the hull.

"Hutch!" Vin hissed again, snapping his partner from his thrall. "Let's not answer and just get going! There's no way they can hold us out here! It's 120 light years away, and we're out of their jurisdiction!"

"Hutch," came the calm voice over the comlink. "Assuming you are the captain of the vessel, I am required to inform you that Centaur Space is sovereign out to 200 light years. And we can hold you until we send a ship. Please, avoid all of this and return Jenny. You'll be allowed to continue on afterwards."

The incredible statement jarred Hutchins into action. He pulled Jenn to him and pressed a bladeless hilt to her neck. Jenny gasped as it touched her infected skin. She'd best prepare herself to act quickly, so she force-transposed the sine wave for ultraviolet light and tri-sected the mantissa.

"Listen to me! I've got a holoknife at her throat. Release us now or I'll cut her! I swear!"

"We understand, *Blue Scout*," came the meek reply. "I'm sorry, Jenny, but we must ask you to return home on your own."

"I understand," Jenny replied quietly. "Tell mom and dad I love them." She almost said Nick, too, but changed it slightly. "And tell Nick thank you."

"Yes, of course, Jenny. Centaur Space Control out."

There was a slight click as the comlink went dead. Instantly, the ship stopped vibrating, and the stars turned into colorful lines as the ship returned to 40000 FTL.

Jenny sighed. She'd hoped it wouldn't come to this. She'd hoped these two men would be reasonable. She took the one-dimension image of the mantissa and decay, coded eleven zeros, two fives and six twos; then connected the seventh two to her hands and waited.

"Don't even think it, kid," Hutch said in a low growl, anticipating a hidden message in her exchange with CSC.

"I'm sorry, Mr. Hutch," Jenny said, and touched her fingers together lightly, completing the BeThere spell.

Instantly, she teleported to the other side of the small bridge. Both men spun around, not seeing her at first. She was most unhappy about causing them any confusion, but she needed to make sure she was all right, too.

"Mr. Hutch. Mr. Vin," she pleaded, raising her arms waist-high. There was a flash of light, and two portals into ireality opened just in front of her hands. "Could you *please* turn the ship around? I'm scared I might not do this right."

They lunged at her, but suddenly fell back as though slipping down a steep slope, the recipients of a HeldBack program.

"I'm so sorry!" Jenny said. She'd forgotten to cast her Haven spell. Despite the error, she nonetheless inserted her hands and arms into the portals.

"What are you doing?" Hutch demanded.

"I . . . I think I'm casting a Rebound spell on the ship," she answered, "but I have to program it from the beginning, and I never have."

"Rebound?" Vin asked. He began edging along the ship console. Hutch was slowly moving the other way.

"Uh-huh. To take me home." She went quiet for a few seconds to better see the lines of the ship's singularity and Centaur sun. She was pretty sure she needed to use a translucent folded ellipse—or was it a transparent one? She couldn't remember! What had Mrs. Handsman said? Translucent for sent; Transparent for rent.

She glanced at the two men just in time to see them floating at her slowly, having canceled her HeldBack spell by turning off the ship's gravity.

"No!" she screamed. The two portals into ireality began tearing at the edges. If they touched . . . . "Stay back! I'm having difficulty holding the spell together!"

Hutchins laughed, but it was a mean laugh. "We're not going back, kid, and neither are you. You're helpless right now. I know enough about Cheats to know they can't cast two spells at the same time. And I know you won't hurt us, that you'll die before you do." He laughed again. "Too bad for you it don't work both ways."

"Hutch," Vin said hesitantly. "This is going too far. We can't hurt her!"

"Shut up and grab her!" They were less than two meters away.

"Stop!" Jenny cried. The portals tears were less than five centimeteres apart and growing closer. "I have to complete the spell!"

"Then cancel it," Hutch said, reaching for her.

"I don't know how," she said quietly as the last spectral barrier was eaten away. "I'm sorry."

There came another blinding flash as the portals touched. Immediately it began to round out and enlarge. The only thing keeping ireality from destroying ship and the two men were the tiny hands of young Marks girl.

Stooping down so the now unconscious form of Hutchins didn't hit her, Jenny held onto ireality for dear life. Vin had already floated by behind her. He too was unconscious, both their minds having shut down when hit with the incomparable light of ireality. Jenny's obsidian eyes, however, had no difficulty in adjusting. And her body, so frail in spectral reality, showed its true strength to live in two realities at one. That only bought Jenny time, though. It didn't solve her . . . .

Abruptly, it came to her. It was translucent! Knowing she could not hold such a large portal open for long, Jenny quickly found the correct chrono string. It vibrated gladly at her touch and cheerfully told her that time was sending them in a direction away from home. Jenny coded in 97 fives, 2 threes, 131 twos, 19 ones and 23 zeros. The code string glowed with life as it bound to ireality. Jenny guided it to the chrono string and braided it to spectral reality. Satisfied, she triggered the program.

The portal vanished abruptly, and the star lines stutter-stepped as the Rebound spell took hold. The ship's spectral direction was now mirrored. She'd done it! They were going home!

Jenny looked fearfully at the two men, but they were still unconscious. She eased them quietly into Sleep; then cast a Haven spell to keep them calm.

The comlink beeped.

"Centaur Space Control to *Blue Scout*. Acknowledge, please."

"Hi!" Jenny said to nothing in particular. Fortunately, CSC was using Talk, so she didn't have to work the comm panel.

"Jenny!" came the relieved voice. "Are you all right? We see your ship is returning. Did you need help?"

"Yes, please," she asked quietly. "Mr. Hutch and Mr. Vin are asleep right now. I can keep them like this until we get back, but could an adult get on the ship and fly it?"

"That will not be a problem, Jenny," was the now cheerful voice. "We will have a pilot rendezvous with you in five hours, okay?"

"Okay."

"By the way, we're all proud of you here, Jenny. You cast a successful Rebound spell. You didn't get discouraged; and most importantly, you treated Mr. Hutch and Mr. Vin properly by not hurting them or inconveniencing them more than you had to. You're quite a young lady."

"Thank you," Jenny replied, blushing. "Only it was Nick who really saved me. I just helped a little."

They said good-bye. She went to the pilot's chair and sat down, pulling her legs up. Jenny glanced over the instruments, but they didn't make much sense.

After all, she was only ten years old.

* * *

AUTHOR'S NOTE:

*i* (a single, lower case italicized i) is the mathematical symbol for the square root of -1 (negative one). In its most basic function, then:

$$i *** i = -1.$$

Considered an imaginary number, *i* can nonetheless be proven to exist by association and inference. Its existence is also required because *i* is used to solve proven theorems in our physical laws.

Since it exists, logic dictates that it can be placed on a line relevant to other, real numbers. Yet it can't be done. Counting to *i* would be akin to pointing to last Wednesday—possible, but far beyond our comprehension.

At least, far beyond the comprehension of *homo Sapiens*.

# Outside The Lines

Earth date: May 9, 3062
Centaur date: Marks Matrix: 70th Remembrance, Tier 4*i*, 395th Vibration of Chronostring 6947; 8amber8 T shading. (2nd reality expression, simplified for linear cohesion to assist in non-*homo Magicus* comprehension.)

"You say good-bye first."

"No, Nick," Jennifer Navarra shook her head, causing the vibrant zebra breeze to quiver and laugh through her long, long, blonde hair. "I said good-bye first last time."

"Uh-uh," Nick replied in playful taunt, his warm, sparkling eyes putting a fine shade of lilac over everything in their acre of ireality. "I said good-bye first last time."

"All right," Jenn laughed, always enjoying their little sign off dance. "We'll do it together."

"Okay. You remember how to find me in the puterverse?"

"Yes," she said, but added with a pout. "It won't be the same, though."

"I know, but at least we'll sorta be together then." He lifted her chin up and gently brushed her lips with his, making Jenn think of cold rushing water that shimmered through her soul, warming it with bright blue fire and freshly picked apples. "And maybe you can get to their moon some weekend, and we can cast together there."

"All . . . All right," Jenn stammered. How much she missed him! She hugged him long and hard, then stepped back. "One . . ."

"Two," Nick counted, waving a small good-bye before raising his slim, muscular arms over his head.

"Three," Jenn said, waving back. She closed her eyes and lifted her arms above her head, crossed them; then brought them down, canceling the ireality spell.

She opened her eyes and saw only the bulkhead of her quarters, located on the eleventh deck of the long range passenger liner *Forever*, one light year from Earth and over six thousand light years from home.

She watched the air in front of her until the last vestige of her spell had faded.  Mounted on the bulkhead behind the now vanished portal was a simple picture of a wiener dog floating in a space ship while the people comically tried to corral it.  Colored by her friend, six year old Bobby Dietrich, it would probably be considered a work of art by his mother; but it wasn't really all that good.  What Jenn liked about it—in addition to knowing that her mounting it made him very happy—was that virtually every color marking he'd made had drifted outside the lines of the drawing.  She liked that he wasn't bothered by it.  He even thought it added to the drawing.  She agreed with him.  As a little girl growing up on Centaur's Heart, Jenn had always colored outside the lines.  And as far as the way she was living now, well, she thought, that's coloring outside the lines, too.

She was homesick but decisive.  Ever since she'd been abducted by Terrans at the age of nine, only to be rescued by Nick at the last moment, Jenn had felt a need to solve the Earth question.

Throughout the known galaxy, wherever humans had traveled, the use of Pentrinsic code had been a boon.  Similar to the Trinary code of the puterverse and the ancient binary code of millennia past, Pentrinsic code was merely the use of numbers to create programming.  The only differences were platform and potency.  While binary and trinary code could program two-dimensional surfaces, such as computer memory or the vast puterverse, the zeros, ones, two, threes, and fives of Pentrinsic code were used to program three-dimensional surfaces, what was commonly referred to as reality.

Pentrinsic was available to everyone, provided the caster was willing to take the years necessary to learn the high mathematics and physical intricacies required. It had been that way for nearly two hundred years. But with the birth of Kerri Marks in 2947, a new race of humans—*home Magicus*—was able to grasp and use Pentrinsic code inherently.

Yet in the three centuries since the first use of Pentrinsic Code—or magic—it had never worked on Earth. Jenn was determined to find out why and had agreed to this four-month journey back to mankind's homeworld as her planet's Student Ambassador to explore the problem. It was a very exciting opportunity—she would also be attending the prestigious Ball Chasers University—but it came with a price: she would most likely lose her own musing power once she arrived and while she remained on Earth. No one knew for sure; a *homo Magicus* being—or Marks, as others called her people—had never been to Earth.

A gentle chiming and soft puff of sweet air pulled Jenn from her thoughts. Turning toward her nightstand, she saw a violet and red question mark shimmering in the holomist.

"Yes?" she inquired quietly.

"Miss Navarra? This is Lieutenant Friedman, the ship's navigator. The Captain sends his compliments and requests your presence on the bridge."

"Yes, of course, Lieutenant," Jenn answered, feeling the excitement of challenge stirring inside her. "I'll be there immediately." She shifted her hands, thought of the final seventeen and a third digits of *pi*, and programmed in seven fives, three twos and zero. A circle of void opened in front of her and the Teleport spell was set.

"Uh . . . If you don't mind, Miss Navarra," the navigator sounded painfully apologetic, "the Captain requests you come through the recreation sphere and use the elediscs."

"Oh," Jenn said, a little surprised. "Yes, certainly. I'll be there in about ten minutes then."

"Very good, and thank you, ma'am."

That seemed odd, Jenn thought as she canceled the spell. Why would the Captain not want her to teleport? No matter, she shrugged. He's the Captain and I'm the passenger. She ran her hands down her loose wrap, and it became less translucent and more clingy. Opening the door to her cabin, she stepped off the ledge and into the air, ninety meters above the surface of the entertainment sphere.

A massive sphere made of aligned titanium around which the ship was built—it was 150 meters in diameter, and its entire interior surface was covered with all the pleasures of entertainment. From musical performances to animal riding to free-fall swimming spheres to gambling tables (from which she'd understandably been excluded), it was all the long-distance traveler could hope for to while away the weeks and months of traveling thousands of light years. It had certainly helped her a lot. Though she spent much of her time with the crew and D'Kint, the ship's muser, she was also known for her hours-long swims.

As always—as required by design—there was no gravity inside the sphere, but Jenn still used Flight to move about. The other passengers required either small gravity thrusters or strong legs and good aim, and she almost pitied them their helplessness. A few knew the Flight spell, but no one could approach her grace and ease with magic.

As she floated quietly across the upper portion of the sphere, many eyes turned toward her. Of the five hundred and eighty passengers on board the *Forever*, she was the only Marks, making her a different and pleasant sight, even after four months. Jenn was thin by human standards; one and half meters tall and massing a meager thirty-five kilos. Childlike in appearance, despite being a grown woman, she had a slight build, looked only moderately matured, and she had thin, elegant limbs. Her shimmering blonde hair was tied back into a flowing ponytail that reached below her waist. She had been compared to the elves of Terran mythology, save that her complexion was too dark and her eyes—which distinguished her race more than anything—were bottomless wells of coal black with specks of cobalt blue. It was said that the only thing deeper than the eyes of a Marks was the depth of their gentleness and peace.

Many adults waved as she passed, while the children shouted their greetings. She waved back to each and every one. Perhaps it was a misplaced sense of royalty, but Jenn had felt regally welcome here on the *Forever*. A curiosity at first since her people rarely moved off their three worlds in the Centaur system, Jenn was quickly accepted and "promoted" to everyone's favorite passenger. Always willing to listen or help, she became a much sought companion by everyone from Captain Mills to little Bobby, who tried so hard to cast his first spell, not quite understanding the difference between him and Jenn.

She arrived at the far end of the sphere and landed on the eledisc. The planed energy sheet flashed once beneath her feet, then lifted her up eight decks to the Bridge. She stepped off, folded her hands in front of her, and waited quietly to be addressed. It was not her place to disturb anyone.

Of course it was D'Kint who noticed her first. Though his casting abilities were very limited compared to Jenn's, his skill was hard earned over the years, and she respected him greatly as muser and friend. The much older D'Kint, in turn, adored Jenn as a doting father does his daughter, feeling a kinship in her that he was grateful she shared. He crossed the bridge, his smile broad and genuine.

"Hello, Jenny." D'Kint bowed and waved her forward through the large and active bridge. All around her, stars extended into colorful lines as the ship—her singularity drive still engaged—swept through space many hundreds times the speed of light. The *Forever* could travel well over forty thousand times faster than light, but was approaching the Sol system and had slowed considerably.

"Captain Mills? Miss Navarra is here."

At the sound of her name, several heads turned, their faces lighting up with warm thoughts. Jenn felt herself blushing at the kindness she felt. Though Marks people were not psychic, there were many elements of reality that stretched into ireality; emotion not being the least of them.

There came a darker tugging thought, and Jenn sensed a fear to her right. Standing there was a group of five people, uniformed in the Terran militia colors of gray and green. She'd heard that Earth always required a presence on ships entering within two light years of the planet, but was unaware they'd come on board. Perhaps it was for their comfort that Jenn had not teleported to the bridge. If that were so, she would need to try to keep them at ease.

"Miss Navarra!" the Captain's tone quickly washed over any tension. "Thank you so much for coming here. I'd bow, but I'm required to keep my chair when entering the Junkyard."

"Of course, Captain," Jenn said in her quiet voice while bowing at the waist. "It is my honor to be here. How may I serve you?"

There came another ripple of fear and—and—something else from the Terrans. Jenn wanted to look a little deeper, but the Captain was speaking.

"As we talked about earlier, we're entering the area known as the Hoboken Junkyard. Did you get a chance to read up on it?"

"Yes, Captain. The *Hoboken* was the first ever faster-than-light ship. It was launched over eight hundred years ago in 2245; but due to damage incurred while going through the Sol system's asteroid field, the ship imploded and exploded when it generated its ball, creating the Hoboken Junkyard just outside of Pluto's orbit."

"Perfect as always," Captain Mills nodded, making Jenn blush again. "The Junkyard's been spreading ever since and for the past five hundred years, we've been helping it. The idea is, the bigger it is, the thinner it is, and the less chance there is of hitting a piece. And for the past two hundred years, every ship's muser is required to use his or her magic to hasten the spread. Commander D'Kint here has done it eight times in the last three years.

"Only thing is, the Junkyard's too spread out for even musers to do much more than a couple pieces. We're hoping you can use your inherent abilities to move a larger section."

"I am only too willing to try, Captain."

"Thank you, Miss Navarra." The Captain's voice sharpened slightly. "Helm! Position, course and speed."

"We are on the primary ecliptic approach to Sol system, point eight light years out and slowed to 700 FTL, sir. We'll be reaching the Junkyard in less than five minutes."

"So about an hour to Pluto." Mills said. He nodded at the crystal clear hull in front of him. "Go to it, D'Kint."

"Yes, sir." Winking at Jen, D'Kint moved to the open casting section forward of helm and navigation and raised his arms.

"Pax," he intoned, and the area glowed a gentle red, the Haven spell keeping him focused and sending a pleasant wave of well-being over the entire bridge.

"Midklyian bot hadina."

Moving his hands so they seemed a blur, Jenn watched in fascination as he slowly opened a breach between realities. His casting was so very different than hers. She felt his straining and wanted to help but knew their magics would not be compatible. For magics to work for humans, mass was required. While Marks people could use mass, it was not required. Nor was it used in the same way, which was the second lesson learned in kindergarten school, right after learning how to count to *i*.

This was D'Kint's realm, Jenn reminded herself. He knew what he was doing.

Five minutes later, it was obvious to all he knew what he was doing. Floating a hundred meters in front of the ship was a huge cube of yellow and white energy, held in place by the willpower of D'Kint. Though he was nearing exhaustion, there was no doubt in anyone's mind that he was still in control.

"Bin doucku Lat!" he commanded; and in a silent explosion, the cube suddenly shattered into five shafts, each stabbing out in different directions, each bolt assigned a target of ancient and destroyed starship that it would fling ever further out into space, thinning out the Hoboken Junkyard one more minuscule step toward oblivion.

The bridge lighting dimmed, and D'Kint sagged back, utterly exhausted. Worried for her friend, Jenn force-transposed the sine wave for ultraviolet light, trisected the mantissa, decay coded eleven zeros, two fives and seven twos, and instantly appeared at D'Kint's side. The BeThere spell didn't have the range of Teleport, but it worked much faster. She pulled up a cushion of soft air under him and cast a Restore spell, keeping it limited to just him. His body glowed a gentle pink.

D'Kint blinked a couple times and looked up at Jen. Seeing the concern on her face, he smiled.

"I'm fine, Jenny." he took a deep, surprised breath. "Rather, I'm more than fine! I feel I could cast again."

Jenn laughed, "I wouldn't just yet, D'Kint. You cast a marvelous spell, but you need to rest now."

"Miss Navarra!" the razor edged tone came from the eldest of the five Terrans, a man with a deep red face and most rigid posture. He was staring at her with anger and hatred. Hatred? No, that could not be right, Jenn thought. Still, he was clearly upset.

Startled that her actions had caused such disapproval, Jenn crossed over to the man and bowed deeply.

"I apologize for causing you anger, sir," she said contritely while looking at his feet. "I wasn't aware that seeing magics disturbed Terrans."

"You don't frighten me, Miss Navarra," he replied, taken somewhat off guard by her meekness. "I just don't want you foolishly wasting your energies flitting about the bridge and performing minor medical . . ."

"That will be enough, Major Datsko," Captain Mills was polite but firm. "You're scaring Miss Navarra."

And he was, too. Jenn had no idea where the major's anger was coming from, but it was clear from the burning on her back and the sour touch in her mind at whom it was aimed. Perhaps, she thought, I could still make amends.

"I—I'm sorry, Major," she stammered out. "I did not mean to mislead or offend. My spells do not require energy. Please, allow me to repay you for my rudeness."

"Just do your job," he replied gruffly, slightly mollified by her acquiescence and substantially put off by her frail will.

"Of course, sir."

Jenn straightened and looked to Captain Mills.

"If I may have the caster's circle, Captain?"

"Of course, Miss Navarra," Captain Mills' voice again washed away the tension and made her feel safe and cared for. She admired him for his ability to not disown his intense and darker emotions but rather to use them only as needed, all the while showing and encouraging his gentle, fatherly side.

Jenn walked to the caster's circle, brushing her hand along D'Kint's arm as he made his way slowly to the Captain's side. Standing in the center, she took a deep breath and thought about how white her sun's star was and what that whiteness would do to the manmade singularity that pulled the *Forever* through space at incredible speeds.

"Captain!" Jenn heard the pilot call out behind her, "we just dropped to 600 FTL!"

"What's the ball mass and position?" Captain Mills said. Jenn felt his mind sharpening at the unexpected challenge. Good, she thought. Once he understands I'm attaching my code to the singularity, he'll calm the others.

"Ball mass and position is unchanged at forty-five point oh oh one six percent mass and two point one six eight eight five meters forward of the bows."

Understanding came quickly.

"Very well," Captain Mills said calmly. "Miss Navarra is using the extra energy. Maintain mass and position and continue monitoring speed."

"Aye, aye, sir."

"Pax," Jenn said quietly, casting a Haven spell.

A gust of air and light burst from her, spreading through the entire length of the 500 meter long ship, coating every living thing with the gossamer touch of peace. Even the Terrans found themselves relaxing and thinking calmer thoughts.

Jenn noted the center of the ship, the center of the singularity and the center of the Hoboken Junkyard. Two glimmers appeared waist high in front of her. As she found each center, the glimmers increased in size and activity. When the final center had been aligned along the *i* axis, she inserted a hand into each glimmer, pushing them in up to her elbows. Somewhere inside was the absolutely right chronostring.

She began plucking each of the strings, causing a gentle wash of music, color and scent to ripple through the ship. Without discernible source, the sensations would be very confusing to humans, so an anchoring spell was required to keep the five reality senses calmed: hence the Haven spell.

"550 FTL and dropping," the pilot called out from a great, great distance.

Far sooner than she expected, Jenn found the correct string. She plucked it tentatively. It didn't make the sound color she was expecting, so she plucked it again. It still wasn't what she was expecting, yet it seemed right. And in ireality, she knew, what *seems* is what *was*.

Her face lit up suddenly. Of course! As happened too often, assumption had led her astray. As wise and kind as the humans were, they had been trying to answer the wrong question for five centuries. She opened her eyes.

"Captain?" Jenn asked aloud, still with gentle tone but now also with a confidence and strength long hidden. Those watching were coming to the realization that she was in her element now, and it was a thing they could never comprehend.

"Yes, Miss Navarra?" his voice was much closer to her than the pilot's had been, for Captain Mills was a well-centered man.

"I fear I must undo some of my peers' efforts so that I may better serve you and Earth. Am I permitted?"

"No!" came the brittle answer.

"Yes," came the firm answer, Captain Mills instantly canceling out the hollow authority of Major Datsko.

"Thank you, Captain."

She turned to Major Datsko, and the immeasurable depths of her eyes froze him in position. The obsidian drew him into her and revealed to him her concern and gentleness while the blue specks gently demonstrated her power and understanding to accomplish what she wished.

"Do not worry or be concerned, Major," Jenn reassured. "I have the correct string now, and I can sense the answer so vividly. No offense, kind D'Kint."

D'Kint chuckled. Here she stood, thirty years his junior, yet many centuries his superior; and she wanted *his* blessing.

"None taken, Jenny," he replied. "Now go to work and do your people proud." He paused, curious, "What are you going to do?"

Jenn gave a playful giggle.

"I'm going to color outside the lines."

Jenn turned forward again, closed her eyes and began programming. Fifty-three ones, twenty-three zeros, thirty-seven twos, eleven threes and thirteen fives.

"400 FTL and dropping."

Sixty-one zeros, two fives, twenty-three twos, twenty-three threes . . .

"200 FTL and dropping."

Seventeen zeros, sixty-seven twos, a single one, nineteen fives. . .

"100 FTL . . . 50FTL . . . 30 . . . 20 . . . . Captain, we're approaching ball destabilization threshold!"

"Maintain ball mass and position," the Captain's voice was as solid as time-mounted granite.

Thirty-one threes, twenty-nine fives, forty-seven twos, seventy-three zeros, ninety-one ones . . . .

"Aye, sir. 12FTL . . . 11.2FTL . . . NINE FTL!" came the pilot's incredulous voice. According to the laws of physics, it was impossible to travel faster than the speed of light but less than 11.2 times the speed of light. Universal constants dictated an instant jump from the speed of light to 11.2 FTL.

"Four FTL . . . Two FTL . . . Subspace . . . Captain," came the awed voice of the pilot, "we are dead in space."

It was a surprise even for Captain Mills. "Ball mass and position!" he barked.

"Unchanged," came the reply. "I—I don't know how, sir—well, I suppose I know how, but not exactly." His voice tapered off, and he stared at the small woman in front of him.

Jenn started building her matrix, pulling the chronostrings out and wrapping them around and in ireality until they began glowing brightly, spilling over into reality. The matrix needed to be 4283 by 29 by 113 by 8amber8 T shading by—and this was the hardest dimension—sixteen. It was the introduction of a non-prime number that would cause Jenn the most strain.

Behind her, alarms suddenly started screaming in protest.

"Incoming!" shouted the Sensor Officer from his station.

"Location!" Mills ordered.

"All over, sir! Hundreds . . . No thousands of particles."

"Size and speed?"

"Nothing larger than a meter, but thousands at just discernible size. The count is up to half a million now."

Jenn began filling the matrix. Having established the when and how, she now needed to create a temporally null cohesiveness.

1019 zeros, 3547 ones, 1373 twos, 2129, threes, 571 fives . . .

"Impact in five sec. . . Wait! There's a change of course, Captain. One kilometer *in front* of the bows!"

Captain Mills frowned and glanced at the Marks girl. No, woman, he reminded himself. She was fully grown despite her size and appearance. Certainly Jenn knew that anything brought to the bows would be consumed utterly by the singularity of his ship. Startled at the thought, he shook his head in disbelief.

"She's collapsing the Junkyard!" he stated with complete and incredulous certainty. "She's pulling it all together in front of our ball to have it sucked in."

4297 zeros, 3259 ones, 653 two, 4391 threes, 3301 fives . . .

And so she was. But then it became apparent that the collecting mass wasn't being immediately sucked in. Every person on the bridge turned in wonder to watch the impossible take place.

4261 zeros, 7369 ones, 5591 twos, 1297 threes, 1009 fives . . .

Slowly but surely, the crew and passengers of the *Forever* watched as the *Hoboken*, the first ever faster than light ship made, was slowly rebuilt before their eyes. Its keel laid 819 years earlier in 2243, launched in 2245 and destroyed only weeks later when it failed to contain the singularity it generated—a precious piece of mankind's past was coming to life again.

5701 zeros, 23 ones, 6791 twos, 4001 threes, 3011 fives . . .

"Sensors to maximum!" Mills suddenly shouted, breaking the eerie silence that had transfixed the crew. "Scan every millimeter of that ship!"

7741 zeros, 2767 ones, 7919 twos, 4931 threes, 3469 fives . . .

The ship lay completely reconstructed before them now, floating on an even keel, undamaged. It seemed poised, as if eager to generate a ball and erase forever its doomed place in history.

7883 zeros, 7883 ones, 7883 twos, 788 . . .

Jenn opened her eyes, startled. The ship was undamaged! That wasn't right. It had sustained damage going through the asteroid field, eight days before generating the ball. And she was bringing it back from the time only one day before its destruction, a full week after traversing the asteroid field. So where was the damage?

Looking deeper into the ship, she sensed a presence—dark, evil and cold. It sickened her to her stomach, and she felt it lashing out toward her. Even as it did, she realized it was both alien and harmless: alien because it was from the puterverse; harmless because it was merely a ghost. It howled in fury and frustration at being discovered, but it also howled in futility. Though its existence was blurred to her because of its use of Pseudo Trinary Code, she could still see it had come to its just end, and existed no more.

So the *Hoboken* had been murdered, Jenn thought. Why or by whom she had no idea. She could have delved deeper and perhaps found the answer, but it was not her place to reveal this kind of Terran history. The entity's ghost would have to go back to where it belonged—lost in time, warped by myth and destroyed by stories untold.

"Captain, if you are finished with your scans, I must release the ship to your singularity." Though still strong of voice, Jenn was clearly tiring.

Captain Mills glanced at his Sensor Officer, who nodded his head. "Whenever you are ready, Miss Navarra. And Jenn?" Jenn's attention caught at his unexpected use of her first name.

"Yes, Captain?"

"Thank you for letting us see this."

She blushed and dipped her head slightly, embarrassed, "You are welcome, Captain."

Spreading her arms, the two rifts opened wide, joining into one portal that throbbed with light. To the crew, it was an astounding sight of colored lines, pulsing strings and heart stopping music. Painful to watch, it was also compelling, and their attention was pulled from the *Hoboken* to the portal. Shielding his eyes but still staring into the place Marks people called ireality, Captain Mills saw what it was to color outside the lines.

7883 fives . . . 4243 fives . . . 1913 fives . . . 239 fives . . . 47 fives . . . thirteen fives . . .

The portal was now blinding as the chronostrings realigned, and Jenn directed impossibility to its proper place while allowing certainty to once again flow unimpeded. Seven fives . . . two fives . . . zero fives . . .

i.

The portal vanished and inside the caster's circle, looking tired but calm, was Jenn. She smiled quietly at the Captain while D'Kint went to her side to assist her as she had him.

Captain Mills smiled back at her, then lifted his eyes. The *Forever* was back at 700 FTL. The *Hoboken* was gone and with it, the Junkyard its destruction had created—all swallowed by his ship's singularity the instant Jenn had dropped her spell.

Though its fate had been the same, Captain Mills somehow felt the *Hoboken* rested peacefully now. It had been brought up from its grave in history, shown to all a final time to be a ship of worth, then lovingly re-interred in a place where memories and the past did not match, where order was an idle amusement for a people that lived there at will. Outside history. Outside reality.

Outside the lines.

# The Cheat

Earth date: May 23, 3062
Centaur date: Marks Matrix: 70th Remembrance, Tier 4*i*, 393rd Vibration of Chronostring 6947; 9amber8 D shading. (2nd reality expression, simplified for linear cohesion to assist in non-*homo Magicus* comprehension.)

Going.

Bringing every last shred of concentration to bear, Jennifer Navarra shoved with all her strength against the shimmering wall of nothing that floated in front of her.

Slowly, as though mired in hardening mud, her hands entered the rift between realities. For an instant only, Jenn felt the relief of magic course through her being, dropping the weight from her overheated body and the blinders from her senses. It was a glorious moment.

There came a sudden pop of scorched yellow flower petals. With a cry, Jenn stumbled against her cabin's bulkhead as the rift that she'd been pressing against vanished.

The growing frustration of the past days was a thing Jenn could feel clinging to her small, childlike body, making her want to constantly wash. When the deep space passenger liner *Forever* had entered the Sol system two weeks earlier, Jenn had begun feeling lackluster and heavy. The ship's doctor couldn't find anything wrong with her, but she could feel her connection to ireality slipping. By the time the ship had swung over to the Uranian moon Miranda to drop off a hundred or so passengers and pick up another two hundred transferring from other vessels for a quick trip to Jupiter, Jenn was having difficulty with her more complicated spells.

She left the *Forever* while it was vacuum docked halfway between Jupiter and Uranus. As a deep space vessel, the gravity variances of planets were undesirable when entire bulkheads were used for living and working areas and no thought was given to natural gravity. It was a tearful good-bye, for Jenn had made many friends during her four month, 6500 light year voyage. She transferred over to the system cruise ship *Many Moons* and had remained in her cabin most of the time, scared of new people and her waning perceptions and abilities.

At Jupiter's moon Io, she still had her simple healing and communications spells—it was the last time she spoke to Nick back on Centaur's Heart—and could muster Flight. But everything else was denied her.

It was after they crossed inside the asteroid field that even her simple magics began failing badly, and she started to feel depressed. She knew she'd lose her Pentrinsic coding abilities, commonly called magic, on Earth. And it was probably for the better that it had been a gradual loss as they went deeper and deeper into the Sol system. But what she'd known in her head she hadn't felt with her heart, and now was the time of bitter realization.

They passed by Mars without stopping. Mars had been the site of a horrifying war many centuries earlier, and it remained abandoned to this day. From there they quickly traversed the millions of kilometers. Now *Many Moons* was in orbit around Earth's moon, and Jenn's powers were all but gone.

She picked herself up from the floor, sat on her bed, and cried. It was a gentle weeping, the weeping of lost love, of unimagined hardship, of failing confidence. Her small body—a slight meter and half tall and even slighter thirty-five kilos—trembled with sorrow.

It was an hour until she disembarked to the shuttle that would take her down to Earth, and she spent most of it crying. Her impossibly deep black eyes, flecked with cobalt blue, had never shed in her life as many tears as they shed now.

But it helped immensely. The ten-minute call to disembark sounded over the atmospeakers, and Jenn felt something awaken life inside her. Terrans lived this way all the time, she thought, ignorant of the joy of living in two realities. Yet they not only survived, they flourished. Couldn't she take from their example and also struggle through? She sniffed and rose to her feet. She doubled up her flowing, waist-length hair and pinned it up around her shoulders; then gathered the remainder of her possessions.

Yes, she could. Though the final vestige of ireality was burning out inside her soul, she would not only endure, she would learn from the very people she came to help and continue on cheerfully. Her desire to help bring magic to Earth—to its people—redoubled, and her earlier confidence returned.

The door toned that the porter had come for her things. She let him in, smiling.

"If you're ready, ma'am," he said, stepping in without a second thought and picking up her bags, not even glancing at her, "I'll take these to the shuttle now."

"Thank you," she replied, folding her hands in front of her waist. "Oh! If I may, I'd like to take my shoulder bag with me, please?"

"Certainly," he replied, picking it off the top.   " Here you . . ."

Their eyes made contact, and the man jerked back suddenly.

"Are you all right, kid?" he said, unable to tear his gaze away from her eyes. "Where are your parents?"

"My . . . my parents?" Jenn asked, surprised. Understanding that he hadn't been told she was a Marks made her suddenly smile. "I'm sorry. I don't mean to be rude. No, I'm traveling by myself."

"Ain't you kinda young?" he asked doubtfully, handing her the shoulder bag with a cautious hand. "And what's with your eyes?"

"I'm twenty-two years old. No, really," she said at his frank disbelief. "I'm from Centaur's Heart. My eyes are like this because I'm a second generation *homo Magicus* human."

"A what?"

"A *homo Ma . . .* a Marks."

His look drifted from frank to blank to cool.

"You're a Cheat, huh?"

The sound of the word made her flinch. Whether intended or

not, it had an abrasive feel that matched perfectly with its definition. Why he had used it, though, Jenn didn't know but was eager to explain.

"Oh, no!" she said, raising her hand to reassure him. But he just turned on her and carried her luggage out the door.

Unsettled, Jenn waited another minute to calm her emotions and let him get to the eledisc. Was this the way it was going to be, then? That seemed unlikely, she decided. The people on the *Forever* had been wonderful companions and friends. Curious, certainly, and full of polite questions about what it was like to be born with the ability to cast Pentrinsic code, but she'd been as curious about them and the way they viewed life and reality. And the few actually from Earth had seemed as pleasant as the others. Yes, this was a single incident triggered by a man not fully aware of outer planet civilizations. And that certainly wasn't his fault.

She gathered herself and left the cabin, feeling much better and pushing down the tiny thought that reminded her that Terrans who traveled deep space were probably different than Terrans who had never *ever* seen magic.

\* \* \*

Gone.

The shuttle was slowly descending to the Lake Michigan space port; and with its entry into Earth's atmosphere, Jenn felt the last vestige of her link to ireality vanish. She smiled slightly, partly from relief that the transition was finally over, partly from satisfaction with herself for weathering the change. From this point on, she knew what it was like for everyone else on mankind's home planet.

Did she still have her math, though? She tried to envision an inverted singularity and the resulting chronowarp. She then applied the plane generated by taking the seventh angle cosecant of a trisected cone that had been created from a five dimensionally rotated equilateral right triangle—impossible without awareness of ireality mathematics—and then combined the resulting geometric paradox to the chronowarp. She then programmed in 13 zeros, 31 ones, 7 twos, 7 threes, and 2 fives.

The mathematical result—a blinding white plane with no thickness that collapsed in on a green-scented hemisphere containing pure water—was firmly seen in her mind's eye. But the physical result—an instant teleportation of the shuttle to the spaceport—did not occur.

She sighed quietly to herself and curled up in her seat. At least she had the math and programming skills, just no way to execute the code in reality. It could have been worse. A lot worse. There was a theory floating around the second generation Marks people that Pentrinsic code would work, but with unpredictable, disastrous effects. Since that wasn't the case, she could start at zero, instead of having to dig herself up to zero first.

The shuttle antigravity thrusters deepened in pitch, and it slowed down abruptly. Feeling queasy because of the unaccustomed changes in velocity, Jenn sat up straight and looked out the window.

The ship dipped below the final cloud cover and she gasped. So beautiful! Blue, blue water sparkled beneath her. In the distance she could make out a shore and a gleaming city. She'd studied up on her Earth geography over the past months and was able to determine that it was the city-state of Chicago. With nearly two hundred thousand people, it was the western hemisphere's fifth largest city. Centuries ago, before the war with Mars and the mass emigration of Earth's population to other planets, Chicago had had over two million souls. Earth now had about one billion people. One billion! Though a fraction of the number Earth's population had once been, to Jenn a billion was still an incredible number compared to the Centaur system's population of ninety thousand.

The shuttle settled into the water, throwing up steam for hundreds of meters, and began docking procedures. Jenn stood up and smoothed her blue, ankle length jumper down around her legs, then adjusted her shimmering yellow body wrap about her waist and shoulders. She felt a little wobbly as the gravity was about ten percent greater than the gravity training the *Many Moons* had used. And it was a third again as much as the *Forever* stayed at the final two weeks of the voyage. Finally, there was no Feather, Flight, or Little G spell to take mass off. Still, since she didn't mass much to begin with, she was comfortable enough.

The other passengers began gathering their carry on luggage. A woman with deep red hair, brilliant green eyes and an athletic look to her reached above Jenn to the overhead compartment and pulled down her own bag. It jingled its delight to see her and settled down on a cushion of air beside her in the large spacious center portion of the shuttle. The woman looked at her and grinned.

"Need me to get your bag?"

Jenn smiled and nodded appreciatively. "Thank you, yes. It's the transcloth shoulder bag." Jenn looked up to the compartment and whistled quietly to it. It chirped back, and let the woman take hold of it.

"Here you go. Guess the Terran shuttles aren't made for runts like you." Her smile took out any offense. "You're Marks, aren't you?"

"Yes," Jenn replied, happy to see such friendliness. "My name is Jennifer Navarra." She bowed deeply at the waist. "Please, call me Jenn. Are you Terran?"

"Nah," the woman replied with a laugh. "I'm Nojuran. That kinda makes us planet buds, huh?"

"Planet buds?" Jenn repeated hesitantly. They were now filing out of the shuttle and making their way to the gravity bound hov that would take them to shore. "That sounds nice, but what does it mean?"

"That means your people and mine fought together in the Six Planets War. Well, not your people exactly, but Marks people are all like your race's founder, Kerri Mark. She saved my people a hundred times over in the war. So we're planet buddies."

"Oh! I think I understand," Jenn said with a bright smile. "Well, I am honored to have you as a friend, Miss . . ." Jenn blushed. "Forgive me."

"Willow. Willow Minshen."

"Then I am honored, Miss Minshen. If there is anything I can do to help or aid you, you've but to ask."

"Call me Willow. Thanks, Jenn. I'd heard that about your people. Always ready to jump in and help. Just like General Marks."

"She goes by Kerri now," Jenn corrected quietly. "She prefers to not look on the past tragedies but instead prepare . . ."

"Hey! Cheat!" a voice snapped behind her. Looking around to see who was upset with whom and why, Jenn was shocked to see a tall, thin man with blonde hair and angry blue eyes looking at her.

"I . . . I'm sorry?" Jenn stuttered out, feeling her ears burning red.

"Move it, kid! Hov leaves in five minutes!" Behind him, several other people were also looking at Jenn with anger. Willow reached out and pushed the man in the shoulder, making him stagger back two steps, wincing. Nojura had a much higher gravity than any planet settled by humans, and Nojuran humans were significantly stronger because of it.

"Lay off her, jerk!" Willow snapped. The man seemed surprised to see Jenn was with someone and backed off, grumbling under his breath. Jenn couldn't make out his words, but his movements and scathing look told her everything.

"I'm sorry, sir," Jenn said, bowing humbly. "I didn't know that I was holding up . . ." Willow placed a firm hand on her shoulder and guided her up the ramp.

"You didn't do anything, Jenn. Don't worry about one brain-celled life forms. Here's the hov now."

They embarked and went to the bows. The hov finished loading passengers and luggage, then swung away from the dock. It rose up five meters on a cloud of antigravity and began moving quickly toward the Chicago docks at the southern tip of the lake.

"So where you headin', Jenn?" Willow shouted over the rush of air as the hov sped along at 200 kilometers an hour.

"I'm attending Ball Chasers University in Madison, Willow!" Jenn shouted back, her small voice all but whipped away by the wind. "Where are you going?"

"Chicago!" Willow yelled. She said something else, but Jenn couldn't hear it, so she began casting Listen. She'd reached the coding for threes before she remembered and broke the spell. She looked up at Willow, embarrassed, and saw the larger woman smiling playfully at her. She motioned toward a table on the forward deck and they sat down. The sound shield instantly cut the outside noise by two-thirds.

"Gotta remember that magic doesn't work here, Jenn. I know," Willow shifted her hands slightly, indicating the beginnings of the Recluse spell, a spell popular among Nojurans. "I travel to Terra . . . Um, Earth, a couple times every year, and I still forget every now and then. I only do small spells. Recluse, Haven, stuff like that. And Free Spirit when I've been . . . ummm, too long without . . . " Willow laughed, winking at Jenn knowingly. "Anyway, it bugs me when I can't cast on Earth. It must be really hard on you."

"I think it's going to be," Jenn said honestly. "I am hopeful I can adjust, though. Perhaps distract myself with my studies. And when I begin making friends, I'm sure that will help."

She looked at Willow, a little anxious, hoping to see approval of her plans in her friends eyes. She was disappointed.

"I hope that works, Jenn. I really do. But I gotta tell you, Terrans are . . . different. They're also pretty stuffy about magic. I don't think . . . . Well, let's just say you've got your work cut out for you. Besides," Willow added with a cheerful grin, "any woman brave enough to come here by herself all the way from Centaur can handle this bunch with no problem!"

Jenn didn't prefer to think of building relationships with Terrans as "handling" them, but she picked up on Willow's intent. Nojurans were a hardy and hearty people, strong in body, mind and opinion. Their planet—almost almost entirely water—was a place of isolated islands and isolated humans. Their towns rarely populated more than one hundred, and they preferred it that way. They lived in small groups or in utter solitude, but they gave away friendships quickly and stuck to them. Their only dangerous trait was a willingness to resort to physical contact if insulted, annoyed, or betrayed. So a Nojuran friendship was easily accepted but seriously taken. Jenn had heard Captain Mills of the *Forever* once remark that if ever they lost their singularity drive, he'd only have to "piss off a Nojuran and he'd have enough energy to travel a thousand light years." A trifle crude, perhaps, but apt.

"Thank you, Willow. I can only hope to do well. It would be a disappointment to return to Centaur in failure."

"Geez!" Willow laughed. "Lighten up, already. You have to start enjoying life now. How old are you? Twenty? Twenty-two?"

"Yes. Twenty-two. How did you—"

"Hey, we're only a thousand light years apart, remember. Two weeks. One, if you go by private yacht. I've been to Centaur's Heart a couple times. And you guys are always poppin' in at Nojura. And we pay attention to our friends. Besides, you're the only generation of Marks so far with the size and eyes."

"That's true," Jenn replied, impressed and honored to be so well known. "After Kerri Marks and the first generation settled Centaur in 3039, all of us born there took on these features. Even the original settlers started drifting toward our race's general physique, though my parents are much taller than me."

"How come?" Willow asked.

"Mainly because this is the best way to exist in both spectral reality and ireality," Jenn said simply. "In much the same way the human form looks so different when accessed into the puterverse, so our forms look different when accessed into ireality."

"Does that mean while you're on Earth you'll revert back?"

"No," Jenn said hesitantly, reviewing the math, knowing the answer but a little doubtful. "This is how I was born, so this is my real physical form in both realities. That I'm cut off from ireality won't change that," she sighed. "I'm going to dearly miss it, though! I thought I'd be able to have some access on Luna, Earth's moon. I tried my magics while out there, and I must be outside their fifth planet, Jup . . . Jup . . ."

"Jupiter."

"Yes, Jupiter to gain any real access. It'll be lonely without Nick."

"Nick?"

"My boyfriend." Jenn couldn't believe how easy it was to open up to Willow. A common Nojuran trait; an easy way with people, unless riled.

"Ah." Willow looked as if she were about to ask an extremely personal question but politely refrained, for which Jenn was grateful.

She was afraid she'd probably answer, which would be completely embarrassing.

They passed the remainder of the thirty-minute trip chatting and enjoying each other's company. Jenn knew she should probably talk to other people—she was certainly getting enough looks passed her way—but Willow was so engaging and so familiar that the trip finished in no time, and the hov was gently bumping against the Chicago dock, the ramp extended down.

"Well, kid," Willow said, standing and stretching. Willow was not too old herself—thirty six—but far more experienced in far more things. "This is my stop. I'll be here for a couple months, so give me a holler when you want to chat or need me to come up and 'explain' things to any troublemakers you run into." She reached down and unashamedly picked Jenn up and give her a huge hug. Willow then set her down, making Jenn give out a small umph! and kissed her on the forehead, under her bangs. Jenn knew the Nojuran Kiss of Trust meant Willow had committed her friendship to her.

Willow remained bent over. A little shy but determined, Jenn stood on tiptoe and kissed her on the forehead in return. Willow straightened, a big grin on her face.

"There!" Willow said, "we're real pals now. You take care, Jenn." She snapped her fingers. Her bag gave out a cheerful yip and began following her down the ramp. Willow gave a final wave, then disappeared into the milling crowd.

\*\*\*

Thirty minutes later the offloading scene was repeating itself, only this time with Jenn getting off in Milwaukee. She'd had her own luggage sent ahead to the BCU dormitory where she was to live, so she had only her shoulder bag. The trip from Chicago had been quick and quiet. It being the last stop, everyone was getting ready to exit, so she still hadn't spoken to anyone.

That was about to change, though. At the bottom of the hov's ramp, she followed the soft white mist that formed a corridor leading to Customs. There were fewer than a dozen non-Sol citizens, so the line was short. Jenn quietly took her place in line and waited.

"Are you a Cheat?"

Jenn turned to the small voice behind her and saw a mother with two little boys. The younger was an infant and in the woman's arms, but the older was standing and staring at Jenn.

Wanting to answer, but uncertain how to go about it, Jenn struggled for the words.

"I'm not sure," she said finally. "Where I come from, we're called Marks. What's a Cheat?"

"A Cheat," the boy replied with utter certainty, "is a little person with black eyes who does scary stuff."

Shocked, Jenn could only stand there, numbed, as the boy skipped along in his description, proud to show off what he knew while having no idea how much his words hurt.

"Mom says that Cheats break the rules, an' they can change stuff and make it different using magic. An' if you're not a good kid, then a Cheat will sneak into your room and change you an' then you gotta be quiet and spooky like them an' then if you're still not good, a buncha Cheats will come and cast a spell on your Mom and Dad and little brother an' then if you're *still* real bad, you get turned into a Wiener dog." The boy winked at Jenn. "That's how come there's Wiener dogs on all the planets. 'Cause it's really lotsa bad kids who got turned into Wiener dogs by Cheats."

"HEY! MISS!"

Jenn jumped, realizing it was her turn to pass through Customs. Her eyes were tear filled, and she had to be asked twice to hold still for a retinal id scan.

"Kid," the official said. "You gotta take the color out of your eyes."

"What?" Jenn choked out.

"Ma'am?" The official spoke to the woman behind Jenn.

"Yes?"

"Tell your daughter to uncolor her eyes." He shook his head. "Teens and their crazy . . . "

"She's not my daughter, officer." Both official and woman looked at Jenn, who was nowhere near as small as she wished she was.

"I . . . I . . . I'm by myself," she said in a small voice. "I'm a Marks. From . . . From Centaur's Heart. This is the natural color of my eyes."

"Geez!" the official snorted, pulling out a tabinal and tossing it on the table in front of him. He waited, staring at Jenn.

"Well?"

"Ummm . . ."

"Listen! If you're going to travel around, you gotta know the rules," he barked. "Understand?"

"No," Jenn's voice was all but gone.

"Not too bright, huh?" he said in exasperation. Behind her, Jenn felt the line becoming restless. "Cheats can't get retinal scans. Your eyes are too weird. An' your DNA ain't on anyone's records, so we gotta go with the old print verification."

He said nothing more, so Jenn hesitantly put her hand on the tabinal. It scanned once, then went dormant.

"Both hands!"

Her breath came in little bursts and her shoulders began to heave, yet Jenn obeyed. She then had the tabinal yanked out from under her by the impatient official. Jenn forced herself to slow her breathing. She ran her palm over both eyes, wiping away the tears. She could fix things. She could.

"What else can I do to help you, sir?" Jenn asked in a wavery voice.

"Just stand there," he replied gruffly, then lifted his eyes to the people behind her. "Sorry folks, but this is going to take five minutes. I gotta special case of id here." He held up his hands at their groans. "Don't blame me! With normal people, this only takes twenty seconds."

It was a horrific five minutes for Jenn. She turned back to apologize; then just as quickly, turned away upon seeing on their faces there would be no reconciliation. Why? she thought. Why does it matter? Yes, I'm different, but I'm not bad. My people are known for gentleness and kindness. Why don't they see that? Is it because I'm only half a person without my connection to ireality? Does that make them only half-people, too?

Jenn blushed at the unbidden insult she'd thought and tried to think of Nick and the comforting words he would tell her when they met later in the puterverse.

Finally the five minutes passed, and with a grudging nod, the official let her through. He gave no more indication that Jenn even existed, for which Jenn was both grateful and hurt. Wiping her eyes a final time, Jenn passed through the sentry barrier.

"Hey!" the little boy shouted after her. "You didn't say if you was a Cheat or not!"

"Of course she is," his mother said in a voice loud enough to cut through Jenn's heart and soul. "Of course she's a Cheat. You can always tell by their rude behavior."

The hallway that led to the Madison shuttle was only fifty meters long, but the shuttle had left before she could stumble up the hallway. She missed it.

She missed the next one, too.

# Miranda's Hope

Earth date: September 1, 3062
Centaur date: Marks Matrix: 70th Remembrance, Tier 4*i*, 393rd Vibration of Chronostring 7283; 6orange1 Y shading. (2nd reality expression, simplified for linear cohesion to assist in *homo Sapiens* comprehension.)

Thrashing, clutching, hot tendrils of solid red mist seized Jennifer Navarra. Every movement she made to pull free of one tendril allowed two more to wrap tightly around her. To one side, always just out of reach, Nick was pleading with her, but she couldn't understand him. And it wasn't Nick anyway, it was Professor Ch'tin. But it wasn't her, it was Professor Gomez. But it wasn't him, it was Mary. But it wasn't Mary, it was . . .

With a cry, Jenn lurched to one side and tumbled out of bed. Mary Powell, Jenn's roommate, rolled restlessly in the top bunk, but then settled into deeper sleep, even her subconscious now used to Jenn's nightmares.

Sweating and near tears, Jenn pulled the maroon bed sheets free of her legs and pajama bottoms and sagged against the lower bunk. With trembling hands, she wiped the sweat from her forehead and calmed herself. For humans, the time between awareness of the nightmare and the change to reality was brief. For Jenn, though, it was a slow process—about ten minutes every waking. Her only solace was the relief the transition brought as her perceptions realigned, washing away the frustration and uncertainty.

Finally more in spectral than dream reality, Jenn stood on shaky feet. Detecting conscious movement, the night clock re-lit and silently indicated it was 1:15 in the morning. Not that Jenn needed to be told; she rarely slept more than four hours at a time. She'd spent her whole life in control of her sleep and dreams. The part of her that was always wrapped by and living in ireality never slept, since sleep was a component of physical reality—or spectral reality, as she knew it to be.

But for the three months she'd been on Earth, ireality and magics were denied her; but the nightmares had moved in to fill the void ireality had left.

Knowing it would be at least thirty minutes before her mind and body could sleep again, Jenn headed to the kitchen. Each floor of the five-story dormitory had a kitchen, and every floor always had one girl that couldn't sleep. The other floors took turns with nighttime kitchen visitors, but Jenn was the third floor's permanent kitchen "ghost".

She walked quietly down the dimly lit, carpeted corridor. Despite being awake because of bad dreams, it was this time of night that she liked because she didn't look as different as the others in the low light. Short, yes. And thin. At a meter and a half and thirty-three kilos, she could and often did pass for a young teen, especially with her physique: fully mature for a Marks woman but quite modest by Earth standards. Her waist-length blond hair—braided by day out of respect for others sensibilities and rolled up at night to keep it from getting tangled during her restless sleep—only added to the illusion of childhood. In truth, Jenn had celebrated her twenty-third birthday a month previously.

But the gloom hid her eyes from those who would be offended. Obsidian with cobalt flecks, Jenn had seen the effect her eyes had on others. New acquaintances who were initially friendly cooled quickly when they identified Jenn as a "Cheat"—a member of the *homo Magicus* race who had an innate ability to program reality using Pentrinsic code. Magic. But since magic was usable everywhere in the galaxy except Earth, Terrans had a very low opinion of those who used it. And Jenn and her people were the living embodiment of magic.

Yet now in the small hours it was different. People who blatantly ignored or even rebuffed her by day would tolerate and speak to her at night. It was a tiny victory—this being accepted by Terrans—

but one Jenn would take. There'd been so few. And tomorrow marked a potentially huge turning point in her relationships with her class-mates. For good or bad remained to be seen.

The kitchen was empty, but the cooling shelves were well stocked. Jenn picked up and set down a half dozen different items, hungry but undecided. She finally chose two bananas. She'd never seen fruit like bananas anywhere, though she was fairly well traveled, and enjoyed eating them.

Relaxing in a study pocket in the lower tier of the eating area, Jenn laid back and studied the stars that glittered in the ceiling's holo-graphic field. There were two floors above her, but the holo was so convincing it seemed as though she were outside staring up into the near endless skies. Not as beautiful as the skies of her home planet, but stunning nonetheless.

She looked in the direction of her home, the Centaur system. It was impossible to see from 6500 light years, but to her imagination it was the brightest star in the heavens. She pulled deeper inside herself and could see Heart, Soul and Hoof, the three planets that shared a single orbit around Centaur. Heart was her home, but Soul and Hoof looked just as beautiful. Flowing around the system, fifty million kilo-meters further out, was the stupendous Mane, the asteroid field that shimmered and twinkled even in daylight. Four months to get here and four months to get back, but not for another four years or longer. Maybe much longer, and not until she had her Masters in Singularity Theory and Engineering, and not until she had solved the mystery of Earth's exclusion to magic.

"Lost in thought?"

Jenn leaned her head farther back and saw her classmate Regina walk into the kitchen area, a large mug in one hand. Of Jenn's fifty-seven classmates, Regina Brock had the reputation of being the hard-est studying. She was often up late at night, refining her answers, expanding her knowledge, and drinking coffee, each enough for five students.

"Yes," Jenn said quietly. "I was just imagining what my home looked like right now."

Regina filled her mug with coffee from the hot-food field and joined Jenn, sitting on another study pocket. The leather sighed against her weight, and the internal grav bubbles quickly adjusted themselves to Regina's preference.

"Miss it, don't you?"

"I do," Jenn replied simply, looking back up into the sky.

"Why don't you go back, Jenn?" Regina asked, with only the slightest of prodding in her voice. "You don't need the degree. Not with all that you can do by cheating."

Jenn said nothing, but her ears burned.

"I'm sorry," Regina apologized. "That's not fair. You can't help being . . . I mean, it's not your fault . . . . Damn! I can't get this right." She took a breath. "I guess I think of you as trying to be one thing when you're already another. Sounds like you can already get a good job, doing . . . You know."

"Yes, that's true, Regina," Jenn agreed. "Marks people—my people—are always in great demand around the systems, especially now that the first generation born on our planets has come of age. But as a people we don't want to be restricted to a single capability. And for us, coding Pentrinsic is not so much what we do as it is an aspect of who we are. Magic is to us what strength is to Nojurans. Or inventiveness is to Terrans."

"I guess I never thought of it like that." Regina said slowly as she mulled over Jenn's words. "That would mean that when you're insulted or ignored because of your che, your magic, we're insulting you and not what you can do."

"Yes," Jenn said in a voice so soft Regina more felt the answer than heard it.

They remained quiet for several minutes, sharing the starlight. A shooting star raced across the sky, chasing Uranus and Venus, which sat just above the western horizon. There was a soft sigh of gravity as Regina shifted herself closer to Jenn.

"Jenn, I'm sorry," Regina whispered. "I . . . I didn't realize. It's just that the math has always come so easy for you. And you're always so quiet and pleasant that it seemed like you were acting superior. That's what we thought."

"Why?" Jenn asked, startled at this sudden gift of revelation.

"Why?" Regina repeated, "because you can do *magic*. You can see other realities. Jenn, you can do things Terrans can't even dream about. Don't you understand how frustrating that can be? And when we see a person like you who is so nice and sweet and quiet about it, it makes a person want to lash out."

"I suppose I'd never thought of it that way, Regina. As a race, we're quiet and willing to serve. It's just our nature."

"How come?"

"Partly it's because while we can program the realities to do many different things, aggressive or harmful spells tear at our souls. One harmful spell can cost the caster—whether a Marks or a *homo Sapiens* muser—years of disturbed thoughts and painful memories."

"I remember studying that during Galactic History class," Regina said, taking a swallow of her coffee. "The Six Planets War of last century. There's so many wars that are happening around the galaxy that this one was just another dry event, despite the fact that it lasted for decades."

"I understand, Regina," Jenn said. "The only reason *i* pay any attention to it is because Kerri Marks was instrumental in winning the war. I know Kerri, so the war is much closer to me."

"She's still alive?" Regina asked. "Wouldn't she be a hundred years old or something?"

"One hundred and fifteen next month." Jenn gave a slow, infectious smile. "I guess that's later this month, since it's past midnight now. The ireality is that she'll be fifty-four. In 3014, she cast an Over Again spell on herself as she slept and started life over as a six-year old."

"You can *do* that??" Regina said incredulously. "You could live forever!"

"Not really, Regina," Jenn replied. "The Over Again spell does regenerate your body, but it also regenerates your mind. Although the essence of who you are—your soul—is unchanged, you lose nearly everything. Memories, skills and experiences are virtually wiped clean. In Kerri's case, nothing could have been better. No single person suffered more that she did from the use of aggressive spells. The Over Again spell gave her a much needed—and much deserved—second chance."

They fell into silence again, but Jenn could feel it was a warmer, more friendly silence. Finally, though Jenn wanted it to go on, Regina roused herself from stargazing. She stood and stretched, giving a yawn; then looked down at Jenn.

"Well, gotta finish up in the puterverse and get to bed." She yawned again. "Have to pack for the field trip tomorrow." She gave a quick smile, one that made Jenn's heart trip. "I suppose you're all packed?"

"Ummmm . . ."

Regina laughed, making Jenn think of Willow in Chicago. Now that she'd dropped her cautiousness, Regina seemed a lot like Jenn's Nojuran friend.

"You're always ready, Jenn. I didn't like that about you, but I'm changing my mind." She nudged Jenn's chair with her foot. "Don't stay up too late, okay?"

Regina refilled her cup at the warming field and left the kitchen, giving a behind-the-back wave to Jenn as she did.

Something ever so subtly had changed in Regina's manner, and Jenn sensed she had made a new friend. Perhaps not a close friend. Maybe little more than an acquaintance that wouldn't look at her so coldly.

But it was a start.

*** 

"Welcome on board the ball chaser *Mahlon Stewart*." The Captain's voice was friendly and enthusiastic, giving no hint whatsoever that this was the fortieth training flight he'd done in as many weeks. Despite his graying hair and seamed face, his soul was as youthful as the students he was addressing. Jenn warmed instantly to the man and his kind, sincere tone. "My name is Thomas Castillo, and I'm the Captain." He glanced around at the eighteen students that comprised the Junior class of BCU's Advanced Singularity Engineering Mathematics.

"How many are on a ball chaser for the first time?" He smiled as the majority of hands went up. He looked them over, always glad to see the same excitement on their faces that he held in his heart. He came to Jenn, and his face went still.

"You are Marks?" he said in disbelief and delight. The other five officers and crew on the bridge turned at the question, their faces stunned.

Jenn blushed and bowed, keeping her hands folded at her waist.

"I am, Captain. My name is Jennifer Navarra of Centaur's Heart. If there is any way I can serve you or your crew, you have but to ask."

Captain Castillo bowed in return. "Miss Navarra, I do have a request or two. Since we keep Chief inside the Sol system for the most part, I don't have a muser on crew. I was, however, Captain for the deep space explorer *Galaxy's Edge* and have had the honor of working with your people before. Once we are outside of Jupiter's orbit, I will call for your services." He straightened and a flicker of a smile came to his face. "I also know something of Marks' preferences. You have my permission and invitation to wear your hair down on board my ship."

"Tha . . . Thank you, Captain." he reached up and undid the braids, letting her blonde hair fall in waves of shining gossamer. Jenn couldn't believe the courtesy she was being extended. She then felt a flash of guilt that she'd prejudged the Captain simply because he was Terran. Bigotry, she warned herself, was not limited to one people and need not be apparent to still be ugly.

"We're about to put to, class," Captain Castillo's voice slipped into an instructional timbre. The normal teacher—Professor Gomez for Jenn's class—always remained behind during the five day outing, and the Captain had command of both crew and class. "We'll be following a parabolic course along the celestial northern hemisphere—Sol perspective—and arrive at the Miranda moon scientific outpost in twelve hours. May I ask why the roundabout course? Yes, Mr. Walters."

"Three reasons, sir." Greg Walters was a tall, heavy young man with a defined attitude and well deserved though annoying superior tone of voice. Jenn appreciated his gift with mathematics and trans-system navigational theory, but had been told in no uncertain terms *he* had no liking for her.

"First, the parabolic course allows for the safest route, avoiding all intraplanetery routes and the asteroid field. Second, since a direct path to Uranus would take us deeper into the system and within ten million kilometers of Venus, the gravity variances are minimized with a parabolic route. Third, though the distance is more than twice further overall, speed restrictions are lifted once twenty million kilometers above the Sol ecliptic, so the trip is much faster."

"Well done. You are correct, Mr. Walters." Greg shot Jenn a snide look, as though telling her he was as worthy of the Captain's attention as she. What Greg didn't understand was that Jenn agreed with him.

"And what are the fourth and fifth reasons?"

Greg's face froze and he looked back at the Captain. He was saved from further embarrassment by having Mary Powers speak up.

"A fourth reason would be for safety, sir. In the event of an emergency it is safer for everyone to have the distressed ship outside the system, especially the inner planets."

"Excellent! And the final reason?" No answer came, and Jenn's ears started warming. She knew the final reason, but was terribly embarrassed. Please! she thought desperately, Don't! Not now, Captain! Please!

Captain Castillo noticed her discomfort and smiled slowly.

"I suppose four out of five is acceptable for a first time trip. We'll stop there. Please, take your seats."

The rear wall of the circular bridge was lined with two dozen gravity chairs, an unusual arrangement without a doubt, but the *Mahlon Stewart* was an unusual ball chaser. The twelfth ball chaser by that name, it had an unbroken eight-hundred-year-old commission, transferring from ship to ship, dating back to the days of the man it honored. Chief Engineer of mankind's first manned ball chaser, the *Horizon*, and the man who coined the phrase "chasing the ball", Mahlon Stewart remained the epitome of ingenuity and skill when taming the artificial black hole that pulled a ship for countless light years at fantastic velocity.

In that spirit to prepare future captains and crews of Earth's respected fleet, the *Mahlon Stewart* was a customized training ship, the product of centuries of refinement in teaching the intricacies of space navigation.

"Helm," Captain Castillo ordered, taking his seat in the chair, "lay in a standard northern parabolic course for Uranus. Time for the Chief to stretch his legs."

"Chief, Captain?"

"Yes, Miss Brock. My crew and I call the *Mahlon Stewart* 'Chief', since the man himself was the first Chief Engineer for a ball chaser. Both name and nickname date back hundreds of years."

"SNP for Uranus laid in, sir," the helmsman called out.

"Very good. Engage fusion engines to 5000 kps."

"Speed five-thousand kilometers per second, aye, aye, sir."

There came a deep hum from the ship, but there was little other indication they had started movement. Indeed, the crew continued moving about as though they were still in orbit. Jenn snuck a glance at her classmates and suppressed a smile when she saw the disappointed look on their faces. Captain Castillo anticipated it as well, for he swung around in his chair.

"You're free to move about now. Sorry if we got your hopes up, but there's really not much to tell how quickly we're moving. It won't get much more impressive, either, since we're going parabolic and there's nothing close enough to view. Still, I know everyone likes the sense of movement . . . " He turned back to helm. "Bring up port display. Lock on the Moon."

"Aye, sir."

The port side of the upper bridge wall shifted from opaque to clear, and the class gasped as one as they saw the moon moving rapidly toward them, sideslipping along their port bow. Though most had been to the moon, velocity on the Earth-Luna run was never greater than fifty kilometers per second. Now, going a hundred times that speed, the journey was cut from two and half hours to eighty seconds.

As they watched, the moon came up, then swung away and was soon shrinking quickly. The sight had a captive audience.

Captive save for one. Jenn relaxed back against her chair, the only one still seated, and closed her eyes. From deep within her and fanning quickly through her slight body, ireality was stirring and reclaiming its lost daughter.

"Are you okay?"

Jenn opened her eyes and saw Regina leaning over, her hands on the arms of Jenn's chair, looking at her with concern. Jenn wiped the tears from her eyes and nodded.

"Yes," she said in a voice trembling with emotion. "I'm wonderful, Regina! I can feel my life with ireality coming back!"

"We're clear of the Luna gravity field, sir."

"Good. Accelerate to 50,000 kps."

"Fifty thousand kilometers per second, aye, aye."

Again there was little sensation beyond the audible. The fusion engines dropped further in pitch, but there was no other indication the ship had just jumped to one-sixth the speed of light. Once more Captain Castillo saw the disappointed looks on their faces. Was he so green once?

"Sorry again. And I'll apologize right now for the next jump in about five minutes, when we go to half light speed. It will be no more exciting." He smiled knowingly, thinking back on every class he'd taken out in the past eight years. "I promise you, though, once we engage the ball on Wednesday, you'll more than . . . . "

Jenn's attention faded. She could see the Captain talking, but she could not hear him. He was a mute hologram to her, as were her classmates, their one reality existence disappearing in the wash of ireality as it once more settled into Jenn's heart and soul.

All in, around, through and beyond her, ireality flooded Jenn's being. A brilliant white light of flowers swept her away, soft breezes and an icy black fire of comfort that smelled of a candlelit window pane during a storm while blue-scented winds brushed at the tears of joy dripping from the tall grass. The chronostrings began chuckling and strumming their happiness to see her again and once more the prime numbers that had been dried out shadows of themselves on Earth breathed again and were awoken in her mind.

"Miss Navarra?"

Jenn opened her eyes as though in a dream of her own making. Captain Castillo had replaced Regina, though he wore the same concerned look. She thought it was silly that he should worry about her. Why? All her suffering of the past three months was finally being purged from her soul! She giggled, then giggled again when she saw the Captain's look go from concerned to worried. She felt his upsetedness . . . Upsetedness . . . Was that a word?

"Miss Navarra!"

Jenn's head jerked suddenly as Captain Castillo slapped her in the face. With a cry, Jenn slipped from the arms of the overwhelming ireality and felt again the cold embrace of spectral reality freeze her soul.

Lurching from the chair, she went to her hands and knees, gasping and twitching. Balance! She needed balance! But it had been so long!

"Back off, everyone!" Captain Castillo barked. "Give her a minute. I think she's having a hard time readjusting to her natural state."

"Tell that to the people on Miranda station," came the irritating voice of Greg. Jenn looked up with hazy eyes and mind and looked at him as he stood over her. "She a useless Cheat, Captain! The people on Miranda are dying and she's overdosed on her imaginary reality drug."

Captain Castillo's face went dark and threatening and he stepped up to Greg. To hit him, Jenn was certain. As gallant as the Captain's action was, she didn't want to see that happen, so she raised a weak hand. Several of her classmates gasped as the saw her hand disappear into a shimmering portal of nothing. Jenn clutched at the ninety-seventh chronostring that wrapped around Greg's consciousness. She decorated it with 13 fives and a single zero, then plucked the string. Greg dropped like sack of lard, though Jenn made sure to cast a Feather spell on him so he wouldn't be hurt. Her hand went to the floor again to support her. Balance . . .

"What'd she do to him!??" someone shouted.

"Calm down!" Captain Castillo said in a clear voice. It cut through the growing hysteria and halved it instantly. "She cast what's called a Soothe spell on him. I've never seen one so quick and potent, though. He'll be out for an hour or two, but he's fine. He's a lot better off by Miss Navara's hand than by mine. Now everyone please be seated. And get Mr. Walters strapped in as well." Captain Castillo knelt beside Jenn. She struggled to lift her head, but he put a warm, calming hand on her small shoulder.

"Take what time you need, Miss Navarra," he said quietly. "I have need of your services, as does the Miranda colony. But we need you as soon as possible."

"What . . ." Jenn could get out no more before feeling dizzy and unsettled, but the Captain understood her.

"We've been underway for an hour. We're 645 million kilometers out and have been trying to rouse you from your stupor. About thirty minutes ago we received an emergency call from the Miranda scientific colony. There was an unexpected shifting in the moon's crust, and their fusion plants were destroyed. They're running on backup reserves, but they were damaged as well. The ball chaser *United* is en route but only on fusion engines, like us. They'll be there in seven hours, but the colony only has power for another hour. After that . . . " he paused and smiled wanly.

"As soon as I received the call, I pushed our engines to maximum. I can't engage the ball this close to the system, but our fusion engines can generate about two-thirds light speed. We're four point three astronomical units out, which is the equivalent of Jupiter's distance from Earth." He looked at Jenn frankly. "That's as far as I can get you. The rest is up to you."

Jenn nodded her head carefully. As with the nightmares, the transition was slow but sure. Even better, where the nightmares faded and disappeared into the false reality they had come from, ireality did not fade. Instead it joined with spectral reality and was blending with it. Jenn's stomach lurched, but she kept control. Control and balance.

"Yes, Captain," Jenn struggled to speak. Her words drawled out slowly as though her mouth and throat were numb, but she managed to say them. Carefully sitting up on her knees, she looked at him through tear-filled eyes. "Yes, Captain," she repeated, this time much clearer. "I can help."

Captain Castillo's smile went from thin to sincere. He stood, helped Jenn to her feet and escorted her to the casting circle in the forward section of the bridge.

"Stations!" he called out, releasing Jenn's arm and returning to the Captain's chair. "All crew to emergency stations. Prepare for . . . ." He looked up at Jenn with questioning eyes. She saw his understanding and nodded. "Prepare for the fifth reason we take intrasystem parabolic couses. In about ten minutes you're all going to have something to tell your grandchildren about. Captain out.

"Helm!" he ordered, "bring us to a halt. I want us dead in space."

"Aye, sir!" The deep throbbing of fusion engines pushed beyond their maximum capacities gratefully ebbed.

Jenn's feeling to her body was returning quickly. Apparently, the three jumps in velocity reinserted Jenn too quickly into ireality ,and she'd been overwhelmed, but only for awhile. She was born into and lived in both realities, so for her it was just getting used to the warm embrace of a much missed companion. And now that she and ireality had exchanged intimate hugs, it was time to serve.

"Pax," she toned, raising her arms. A concussion of peace and warm gentleness erupted from her small form as the Haven spell blanketed every soul on board the *Mahlon Stewart*. Everyone felt a calm wash over them. Not induced from without but rather encouraged from within; it was a familiar calm that cleared the head without softening the will.

Opening a large rift in front of her, Jenn carefully pushed both hands in. The light was very intense, which didn't bother her at all but could blind humans, so she quickly coded a Dark Glass program, which would allow everyone to watch without harm.

Pulling back the surface layers of current time, Jenn revealed the throbbing orange and violet chronostrings of what could be and what could never be. The Chief needed to be at Miranda station now. But since 'now' was an infinite variable, more an element of ireality than spectral, Jenn needed to solve for now, and the resulting solution would impact both. She located chronostring 7283 and noted it was 6orange2 D shading. Gently tugging at the 7purple7 F shading of the 7283 chronostring, Jenn braided them together. A wash of surprise and recognition caressed her back as several of her classmates saw the braid matched the one Jenn wore in her hair.

Satisfied the temporal rift was stable, Jenn withdrew her hands and turned toward aft, toward the Captain and her classmates. Despite the seriousness of what she was attempting, Jenn still felt a warm satisfaction in being able to finally show them how much she cared.

Moving her hands in opposing circles, her thumbs and pinkies at right angles, Jenn smoothed out spectral reality. It rippled and parted, opening a portal into the ireality that lay just beneath its surface. Again, blinding energy poured out of the portal; but instead of light, it was heart-stopping blackness that had physical presence. Satisfied she was properly oriented, Jenn began searching for the twinkling points that were Miranda and the *Mahlon Stewart*.

Within moments she found them between the mass and energy planes. The ship's point vibrated cheerfully as it performed the duties for which it was made. The Miranda point was brittle and sharp and jumping around without pattern or purpose. She caressed them softly, singing a quiet song of Soothing.

A second spectral rift—this one a picon and picosecond distant from the first—opened, pouring out a physical white light. Jenn increased the Dark Glass spell to maximum, though again the light didn't bother her. There were now three portals open; one temporal and two physical, one what was and the other what was going to be. A final step remained: coding. Kneeling in the middle of the casting area, Jenn took a deep breath, bowed her head and started.

6143 fives, 1747 threes, 1999 two, 3457 fives, 4001 zeros, 7927 ones, 5 threes, 967 twos, 2221 fives . . . .

The three rifts began expanding abruptly. No thicker than a line, the visible surfaces soon overwhelmed them all on the bridge. They reached the hull and deck plating and continued on unabated.

"Shift to transparent hull," Captain Castillo said calmly.

A soft mechanical beep was heard and the hull went clear, allowing an unobstructed view on the upper port and starboard bulkheads. The portals continued expanding until they were the diameter of the ship.

9293 fives, 14389 threes, 8599 twos, 19571 ones, 10463 zeros, 10079 fives . . . .

The two matched portals separated, with the white physical sliding along the *Mahlon Stewart's* axis aft and the black portal forward. The temporal portal remained stationary, just behind the tiny figure that was motionless on the floor, save for her steady breathing.

14387 fives, 11789 twos, heartbeat, 8117 fives, 12953 threes, heartbeat, 11399 fives, 16981 threes, 6311 twos . . . .

Having reached the bow and stern of the ship, the portals reversed direction and raced toward each other. Alarms began sounding all over the ship,and the comlinks were instantly jammed.

There was little doubt as to the cause. As the black portal passed through the bridge, the *Mahlon Stewart* ceased to exist. Where once was a bridge, there was now open space. As the portal moved through each person, a bubble of protective energy appeared, keeping in a life saving atmosphere. There was no doubt though that the ship was gone. Still the time portal had not moved.

20411 fives, 13553 threes, 12347 twos, 11131 ones, 14207 zeros, 20897 fives, 19681 threes . . . .

The portals finished ravaging the ship and stopped. They remained motionless but seemed ready to pounce.

24043 fives, 22003 threes, 15061 twos, 25111 ones, 32051 zeros . . . . Heartbeat.

Jenn's forehead was burning. Her muscles screamed for release. The difficulty lay not in her recent return to ireality but in the sheer magnitude of the spell while still in the vicinity of Earth. Even at half a billion kilometers, Jenn could feel the planet's dark presence. It pounded her soul and tried to crush her will beneath its weight.

33301 fives, 36473 threes, 24023 twos, 39341 ones . . . .

How could such a beautiful planet cause such pain within the

soul of a muser? Of a Marks? Did Earth itself hate Jenn? Did it want
to attack and expel her the way a body fought a disease?

38377 zeros, 38651 fives, 35267 threes, 39439 twos, 41507 ones,
41011 zeros . . . .

It doesn't matter! she thought with a cry that every crew member
and classmate felt in their bones. I will save her people now. Both
those here with me and those on Miranda. They placed their trust in
me, and I will not dash their hope in me!

42139 fives, 45433 threes, 45823 twos, 45827 ones, 45833 zeros, 45841 fives . . . .

Jenn jerked straight and her arms reached out full. Her eyes
snapped open.

"Now!" she shouted.

The two physical portals spiraled from vertical to horizontal
and flashed into the time portal, pulling everyone with them. It was a
soundless collapse, over in an instant and leaving nothing behind save
a pinpoint of light that burned on its own for several moments before
it too flickered and died.

\*\*\*

"The last shuttle is on approach, Captain," the comlink crackled and sputtered from the power surges of the station's ruined power
stations. In the forty minutes that had passed since Jenn's Alter Now
spell had teleported first the ship and then her crew into orbit around
Miranda, the *Mahlon Stewart's* three shuttle bays had been busy taking in the station's 700 scientists and support staff.

"Very good," Captain Castillo said with satisfaction. He'd just
come up from the lower decks where the injured had been taken. He
stood beside Jenn—or rather she beside him—and smiled at her.
"Stand down from emergency alert and secure for sea once the bay
doors are closed. Lay in parabolic for Earth, best speed." He winked
at Jenn, causing her to look down, embarrassed at the familiarity.
"Make that best *physical* speed."

Jenn looked down from Bay One's observation room. The last
shuttle to carry people was making final approach into the wide open

bay doors. Behind it was the dark surface of Miranda, hanging in front of Uranus's bright blue glimmer, looking like the final coal burning in an eerie fire of turquoise. The shuttle landed and the bay doors closed. Jenn breathed a sigh of relief and turned to the Captain.

"With your permission, sir, I'd like to assist my classmates in aiding the injured."

"'A Marks work is never done', eh?" he replied, quoting the well-known saying. "Permission granted." She bowed quietly at her dismissal and turned toward the door.

"Miss Navarra?" Jenn turned back. "I've been talking to your classmates. They're very impressed with your skill and magics. Even Walters. I don't think you'll be hearing the word 'cheat' again anytime soon.

"But to a person they were most impressed with your attitude. Despite the foul treatment you've had to endure since you've gotten to Earth, you didn't hesitate for even a moment to save people who until a few hours ago would have been just as cold to you as the others. Why?"

She looked at him for a moment, considering. He deserved a truthful answer, of course; and she was satisfied that he could handle it and not think of her as being conceited or arrogant.

"I could never ask that question, Captain," Jenn replied. "For a servant, there is no such word as 'why'."

# Also Available from Peter W. Prellwitz

Horizons

Promise Tide - Book One
TAU - Book Two

2005
Shards: Book One
Shards: Book Two
Shards: Book Three
Shards: Book Four

Redeeming the Plumb

2006
The Angel of St. Thomas
Royal Pathmaker

Printed in the United States
26729LVS00006B/148-189